It's a pretty frightening experience for ... ...he's grabbed and threatened by a sinister woman motorcyclist who gives her a strange message for her grandad. Confused and shaken, Paula is shocked to discover that her grandad – a hard-working East End cab-driver – has got mixed up with a local gang of ruthless crooks. Innocent witness to the gang's robbery of a jeweller's shop, and in possession of a vital piece of evidence, the old man is in a dangerous and frightening situation. Both the police and the crooks desperately want the evidence – and the crooks will stop at nothing.

When Grandad dies suddenly, Paula finds herself alone with an impossible choice to make. She knows she should go to the police and help put an end to the gang's criminal activities. But she also knows that to do this would be to endanger her family.

This new novel is by one of Puffin's most exciting authors. Bernard Ashley was born in Woolwich, South London, in 1935 and educated at the Roan School, Blackheath, and Sir Joseph Williamson's Mathematical School, Rochester. After National Service in the R.A.F. he trained as a teacher. He is married to a teacher and has three sons. He lives in Charlton, not far from the scene of his early childhood, and is Headmaster of Charlton Manor Junior School.

Bernard Ashley

Running Scared

Puffin Books

Puffin Books, Penguin Books Ltd, Harmondsworth, Middlesex, England
Viking Penguin Inc., 40 West 23rd Street, New York, New York 10010, U.S.A.
Penguin Books Australia Ltd, Ringwood, Victoria, Australia
Penguin Books Canada Limited, 2801 John Street, Markham, Ontario, Canada L3R 1B4
Penguin Books (N.Z.) Ltd, 182–190 Wairau Road, Auckland 10, New Zealand

Published in Puffin Books 1986
Published simultaneously in hardback by Julia MacRae Books

Made and printed in Great Britain by
Richard Clay (The Chaucer Press) Ltd, Bungay, Suffolk

contents

I gratefully acknowledge the debt I owe to Paul Stone, Executive Producer, BBC TV Children's Drama, for his help and encouragement in the writing of the television serial on which this book is based; and I thank Marilyn Fox, Director, and the cast and crew for their integrity and skill in bringing it to life on the screen.

B.A.

one

A trickle of late-afternoon passengers came out of the Underground at Oakwood, waving seasons and throwing tickets into the empty collector's cabin. Mostly shoppers and commuters who'd beaten the rush-hour, they hurried on without breaking step, the last a young man, about twenty-one, with the soft moustache and hard attaché-case of a young executive. He slipped his uncollected ticket back into a waistcoat pocket and walked on with the rest, a bored, fixed look on his face as if he did this every day of the week. Outside the station he made for the large commuter car park, where, passing down a long line of cars, he eventually stopped at an automatic Cortina estate, walked all round it as if he were a sensitive owner checking for marks, and with a final look at the lock he took a key from his attaché-case and opened the door. First go. Smiling now, but not so that anyone would notice, he laid the case on the seat beside him, turned the key in the ignition, put the lever into 'drive' and headed for the exit where the car hit a small bump: at which the attaché-case yawned slowly open to show a hundred other keys neatly bedded in the foam inside. "Shut up!" the young man said, slamming the case tight with a free hand; and turning the wheel to the right he headed out of the car park in the general direction of London's East End.

Three-quarters of an hour later he was gentling it into the alley at the side of Shepherd's Gate's *Empress Bingo*, and he reckoned his own part in the hold-up was just about done. With an even greater care now, avoiding a large black Mercedes and a fiercely shining Kawasaki motor-cycle, he parked the car and gave a confident thumbs-up to the man in the

Patrick jumper, standing waiting outside the old stage door, arms folded minder-style.

"What you get, son?" the hard man asked, as if he couldn't see it.

"What you wanted, only automatic." The young executive slammed the driver's door to give his words a bit more authority.

"Automatic?"

"Yeah, nice car, handles all right: I know these, they're good as gold." He looked up with a hopeful expression on his face. "Shall I show it to ...?"

Ronnie Martin spat into the gutter. "Mr Elkin won't want bothering with you. Gi's the keys, an' on your bike, son."

The younger man, looking a lot less confident now, tossed the keys at Ronnie in a mild gesture of not caring, and turned to walk back down the alley towards the road where the buses ran; while the other stared after him with scorn in his eyes before suddenly pushing back into the building.

The bingo hall was only half-full with players; pensioners, housewives and unemployed out to win a joint of meat: but the size of the house was of no concern to anyone. The bingo was only a front: it was in the back room where the real money-making was organised these days.

"This ain't still one-way with them road works?" Charlie Elkin looked up from the map like the chairman of the board from his annual report. "Only I've got to be sure." Fit and in his thirties, he was wearing a well-cut suit which still managed to show some muscle: a sleek man: smooth, violent, confident – and the undisputed king. And dark, and good-looking, a cockney with a touch of Italian, a one-man Mafia in gold framed glasses who controlled the East End from this nondescript room.

Next to him, blinking and screwing at the watery streets, Fred Barrett was trying to focus. "Where's that you're pointing?"

"Katherine Road." Elkin started at his right-hand man. "Christ, you can't see for looking, can you?" He turned to the woman in the corner. "Got a magnifying glass for Blind-eyes?"

Leila, creaking in her motor-cycle leathers, helped cover the man's embarrassment with a laugh. "Give him a lend of yours."

"Well, it ain't no big disgrace, wearing bins."

"I can see!" Barrett ignored the thick-lensed glasses Elkin was pretending to offer. "Anyhow, that stretch, it's clear now, all the way down to the Barking Road."

"Good to hear it." Charlie Elkin looked at Barrett as if it might have been his personal fault if the road works hadn't been finished. "We can have the second motor round the back in Wakefield Street. Do the switch by the market. There's always people shunting stuff in and out of motors down there."

Leila crackled the pink pages of the *Financial Times*. "That's good, Charlie," she said. "I like that."

"Oh, well, that's all right then! I c'n sleep tonight!"

The woman looked away as a short and secret knock brought Ronnie Martin in on a wave of bingo sound. "Butler's back with the motor, Charlie. Got what you was after, Cortina estate – 'cept the berk only went and got a stupid automatic!"

Elkin shrugged his tailored shoulders. "Same difference, son. Got the new plates on?"

"Yeah, 's all ready."

"Right. I'm putting Butler in the second car, give him a taste of the real stuff, dry out that wet behind his ears."

"Eh?" Ronnie snorted. "Dry him out? He'll wet his little knickers! Anyhow, I sent him home."

Charlie Elkin gave him one of his looks, the sort that said not only who was the boss but what sort of a boss he happened to be. "Then get him back!"

Without a word Ronnie turned on his toes and hurried out of the room, managing not to slam the door. Fred Barrett, though, older and longer in Elkin's service, was sometimes allowed to argue. As a privilege it was a bit like being allowed to swim with a crocodile, but it was one he bravely took from time to time.

"Make me wrong, but I don't see it, Charlie. Butler or no Butler, what's the point of doing a little job like this in the first place? What's it for?" His creased old London face looked across at Leila in the hope of getting some support. "Knocking over a two-bob jeweller's down the road in a Cortina estate? And you Mr Big all over the East End! It don't make sense. I tell you, Charlie, I've got more gold in my gob than he's got down that shop."

But Leila showed where her loyalty lay, the same place where she laid down to sleep, next to Charlie Elkin. "Gold's up thirty pence in here," she crinkled the City pages. "So you watch your gob!"

And Elkin had got up and was circling the map of Shepherd's Gate like a padrone round his estate, his hands waving to emphasise the reasonableness of what he was saying. "I'm showing myself, son. Just because I *am* who I am, and because I'm gonna stay that way. Every once in a while it gets ... necessary: every once in a while I have to let everyone know that when I say pay up they pay up – or else! *Or else*, Fred!" He looked across at Leila to make sure she was nodding. "And for that two-bob jeweller Wisener, today's the else, son."

"I still don't see it," Barrett persisted.

Elkin suddenly stopped in front of him and whipped off his expensive frames. "Then I'll definitely have to make you an appointment to see my optician." He stared straight and fierce into the older man's face, held it till he lightly smacked at a cheek with his fingers. "Now," he said, "let's have a look at the motor." And replacing his glasses, he led his way outside.

"Unlucky for some ..." the bingo caller announced.

"Thirteen!" the hall responded.

10

Elkin swivelled to Leila and smiled, nothing more than a creasing at the corners. "They can say that again!" he said.

The bus queue outside Goldings Comprehensive School was its usual push and shove, pushing across the pavement to the railings and shoving with elbows and plastic carriers towards the front. With one bus every twenty minutes, the drivers preferring to stop short and turn round rather than make the school pick-up, it was a frustrated scramble most afternoons. But horse-play, insults and a bit of boy-girl business usually helped the time to pass.

For two girls in the queue, though, for Paula Prescott and Narinder Kaur Sidhu, the interval between buses seemed endless, the appeal of banter, nil. Because Narinder's eyes hadn't seemed to leave the ground for days, and now Paula's were starting to look somewhere else for friendship. Seven years together might have been a long time, but it was as if the older racists had got at them and suddenly the repartee, the quick laughs, the lightning looks which said a lot, all these had almost gone. But since colour had never come between them, what it was all about was hard to understand for Paula; while Narinder didn't have any option but to keep quiet about something she didn't understand herself. So there was this depressing buffer in the middle of the queue, two girls past whom the shouts and passings-on couldn't run, a deadening effect like wet blankets at a party.

The bus eventually arrived to a mix of cheers and abuse, and a surge forward which threatened to throw someone under its wheels. From the top deck, two pensioners on their way home from the bingo looked out at the queue and pulled faces as the riot clattered up the stairs and rocked the bus on its springs. Narinder and Paula slumped themselves into a seat in front of the old women and noisy pairings went on all around, while Tommy Parsons and Scott Taylor found themselves places as near to the two girls as they could, with only the pensioners between them. Tommy stood up and leaned over, almost knocked a wig out of place. "You comin' out tonight then, Prescott?"

Paula turned in her seat but put her face back to the front again before answering. "No, I ain't!"

"What about you, Nind? Meet me down the bench 'alf-seven?"

Narinder flashed her eyes. She might have been miserable but when the top deck suddenly went quiet she knew she had to reply. "I wouldn't be seen *dead* down the bench with you."

Tommy laughed and leaned over further. "You don't need no dowry to come out with me, you know!"

"No, *I'd* need the paying! Get lost, Parsons!"

Tommy jeered, but the sound was cut short by a look he got from one of the women in front of him. "Got your eye on the sixth-form, then, Nind?" he tailed off: lame words which spun Paula's head so fast to face Narinder that something clicked in her neck.

"Here, is that what all the moody's about? You're not thinking of going out with no-one from the sixth-form, are you?"

"What, with my dad? I'm lucky to go out with my mum sometimes!" And Narinder snapped herself shut in her silence again, staring out of the window, seeing nothing.

But Tommy couldn't let anything rest. "Anyhow, Linda Bradley knows when she's well off!"

Paula laughed loud enough for downstairs to hear. "What, with you? Well off her head, you mean!"

For reply Tommy and Scott whooped in derision and pushed to be first down the stairs, with a hand spare each for sign language at the girls. But it was quiet when they'd gone, and Paula tried for the millionth time to get some sort of sense from Narinder. "Cheer up, Nind, it might never happen!" she started.

Narinder went on staring miserably out of the window. "I think it already has."

12

"Why don't you come home to tea then? Watch my grandad finish that necklace he's making me."

Narinder didn't even have the will to put much into her sigh. "No, I can't," she said, "if it's not all fixed up before ..."

"Yeah?" And Paula turned away to stare into the distance herself. She had tried, her long-suffering face seemed to say, but all she'd got was blanked. And what use were friends if they couldn't tell each other things? She looked round at Narinder again, at the sad, dead expression on her face. And her eyes softened, her head tipped sympathetically to one side. What was it that was changing Nindy from the brilliant mate she'd been into this zombie who'd just as soon stare at nothing as look her best friend in the face?

Paula's house sat neat in the middle of a well-kept row of small dockers' houses in East Ham. Built without garages in the days before people had cars, the road was narrowed by a line of vehicles parked tight on either side, reducing the traffic flow like cholesterol in an artery, and increasing the blood pressure of the people who lived there: a condition not helped by people like the Prescotts with more than one vehicle to manouevre into the space. Paula's father and grandfather were cabbies, so there were two black London taxis parked up at night outside their house.

And this afternoon one of them was still there; Paula's grandfather was giving it a clean at the kerb. It had got to the leathering-off stage where you could see what he'd missed, and as he wrang out his chamois into the plastic bucket, it could be seen that he'd missed plenty: the bottom bits, on doors and wheel guards where his head had hurt when he'd bent down low, and in the middle of the roof where he just hadn't seen. Now, shaking his thick-haired grey head like a boxer after a painful blow Sam threw in the leather and shuffled into the house.

It was after-school time; Paula's mother was home from her

job at the car showroom and Dean was lying across the floor in depths of the long-piled carpet watching whatever moved on the box. Careful with his bucket in the smart, open-plan room – the carefully rough-plastered walls, the veneered bar, the low-lit tropical tank – Sam stepped over the boy's awkward legs and went through into the kitchen area to the sink.

"'Scuse, Doll," he said, "I'm putting more dirt on than I'm taking off."

Dolly threw the last potato into a pan and frowned round at her father. "Then why the devil don't you do what Mick says? Let him run yours through the car-wash? If it's good enough for his . . ."

Sam rubbed at his temple. "He won't want to do that when he gets in. Six hours cabbing's enough for any man." He dropped his hand from his head and slapped his leg hard, the way old, once-active people do when they start getting frustrated with their bodies. "The day I can't look after my own cab's the day I take it back." But his hand had to go back to his head quicker than he'd bargained for. "No, I'm just fed up having to let young Paula down. There's no way I'm up to finishing that necklace tonight, not wi' this mother and father of an 'eadache."

"Oh, Dad, not again . . ." Dolly frowned, little lines which didn't always go away these days. "You know we're out of your tablets, I told you this morning. Why don't you do what I say and see a doctor? Get some proper stuff. Get him to give you a once-over." She tried to smile encouragingly. She'd had her father with her the seven years since her mother died and it had meant extra work; but only now was she starting to feel that he *needed* her looking after him.

"I'm all right. Just an 'eadache now and again." Suddenly he tipped the bucket of fresh water back into the sink. "Blow it," he said, "I'll run it through a car-wash myself. An' I'll shoot down the Boleyn and pick up some Anadin the same time."

Dolly was still staring at him. Getting the dinner could wait while this was sorted. "You sure you're all right, Dad?"

"'Course I am, straight up."

Dolly shifted her weight, pretended to give some attention to the mince. "Dunno if I ought to let you go."

She would have gone on to say something: she opened her mouth for it. But Sam took hold of her shoulders and made her face him. From somewhere he found a faint twinkle. "Oh, yeah, Dolly Daydream? Since when did you start telling your old dad what to do?"

Dolly smiled back at him, found a twinkle of her own. "Since I was about three. Only you was never bright enough to twig it!"

Sam laughed and hugged her, gave her a shake like the start of a comic dance. But with his head over her shoulder she couldn't see his face, or the look of pain that was really getting to him.

At the back of the *Empress Bingo*, between the sessions, things were coming to a head of their own. There was a lot of coming and going, and all so innocently done that if anyone had been watching they'd have probably guessed there was something guilty going on. Towards the end of it, with the stolen Cortina automatic estate parked tight to the stage door and its rear door up and open, Fred Barrett, looking casually about him, came out of the building and threw three large plastic grips into the luggage space. Wearing a long, hooded anorak, his head bare at present so that he could see all round, he watched as another car – a metallic blue Granada – nosed into the alley and parked close. The young executive at the wheel, who was dressed more comfortably than Barrett in flat cap, leather jacket and gloves, slid quietly out and shut the door with a click. Butler stared about, confidently, but if he'd thought he was going inside among the big boys tonight he was mistaken.

"Wait 'ere," Barrett told him. "An' don't make an exhibition of yourself."

In Charlie Elkin's office, the last touches were being put to the raid on Wisener the out-of-line jeweller. Ronnie Martin, anoraked like Barrett, was at the freezer, digging deep beneath the tubs and bars for a sawn-off shotgun wrapped in protective plastic, while Leila Duke was finishing fitting the wig which would change her from Charlie's glamour-girl into a dowdy housewife who'd just lost her housekeeping at the bingo.

"Come on, finish with that barnet, girl. Time you was on that bus," Elkin told her from deep in an anorak of his own.

Leila didn't take her eyes off the careful pinning of the wig. "Thirteen past it goes, I'm all right." And in exactly the right time for taking a trotting little walk in a scruffy mac down to the 58 bus she left the office, carrying something small and heavy in her shopping bag which she definitely wouldn't want to show to the driver.

Watching her go, Elkin had a word with Butler in the Granada. "Right, you might have a bit of bother getting parked up so it's straight round the market where I said." The driver looked at him and nodded. "Sit tight till we get there, then just take the bags as if they was some leather goods you're movin'."

"Gotcha, Mr Elkin."

"All right, go on, then."

He didn't need any second telling, not from Mr Elkin, not from the man who said whether people lived or died this side of London. He took the car out carefully, rolled it in second gear past the others, and joined the rush-hour build-up down High Street North towards East Ham's Wakefield Street. And as soon as he'd gone, Elkin, Barrett and Ronnie Martin, warm in their anoraks and hot with weapons, jumped into the stolen Cortina and headed off the other way towards a jeweller named Wisener at the Boleyn.

two

In one of the shopping streets between Paula's house and the corner where the raid was planned to take place, Narinder's father had set up his small printing business. It had been a greengrocer's when he'd bought it, but there were greengrocers everywhere, it had seemed, while there were very few people prepared to supply the printing needs of a rapidly growing Asian community ... which was handy, as Narinder would have said, seeing that Pratap Singh Sidhu had trained as a young man at the London School of Printing. So he had set himself up. But like plenty of others in difficult times, he was feeling the pinch these days – and not only the pinch of the government's economic policies: there were other things going on as well which were both emptying the till and draining Pratap of some of the courage he'd once been famous for.

Protection, that was the name of the game. The protection racket. The smiling, matey face which threatened a razor if you didn't smile back. Soft words wrapped round hard threats, like muffling round a gun. So the big greengrocery windows were painted black to above eye level, and customers had to ring and be recognised these days before Pratap would let them in. None of which, of course, was any good for business; and wasn't much better for family life, not when it meant that no-one could go out except in the brightness of day, and they all had to give a coded ring to get themselves let back in.

And this was what was depressing Narinder: seeing her dad going downhill, feeling all this edginess at home, and not understanding any of the reasons why except what she could see for herself – that he was running scared of something.

Tonight she had Paula with her, had persuaded her on the

bus after the boys had gone to leave her necklace for half an hour and come and have some tea with her. It was the least she could do, seeing how moody she'd been all day. Besides, she always liked taking Paula into her bedroom, never got tired of her saying how it was special, got a lift every time from knowing it had a style her friend had never found anywhere else. Because she *was* different, and this room showed just where she stood in the world, with its framed picture of Guru Nanak all bright on one side and Bruce Springsteen on the other: with a long-necked sitar propped up against the stereo. And it was her own room, too – Paula always went on about that. Being an only child wasn't always a drawback.

The tea grouts were cold now, and Paula would have to be going, but another family's photo-album is always intriguing, and Narinder's was more than most, especially coming out now: because these Sikh wedding pictures, outdoor in India, showed Nindy's parents as such beautiful, carefree people, like film stars, and very different to the unhappy couple downstairs.

"Here, look at your mum. Weren't she pretty?" Paula's eyes said it all, how it always gives your stomach a turn to see a beautiful bride, that weird feeling at the mix of religion and sex. "Looks happy, don't she?"

"She does there. It's different now."

Paula looked up sharply as if that was it, the reason for the long faces suddenly made clear: as if Narinder was trying to bring it out in the open in these pictures. Was there something up with Nindy's dad and mum in a man and wife sort of way? Was that the problem?

"No, nothing like that!" Nindy's brown eyes widened, she wrinkled her fine nose. "Something else." She waved her arms wide.

"The business?" Paula started to nod, looked relieved that it wasn't family. "My dad and my grandad have bad weeks, cabbing. They wouldn't give a smile to a baby sometimes, neither of 'em."

But Narinder hadn't really stopped shaking her head from the question before. "No, it's ... Paula, it's big: it's ever so big, I know it is!" She dropped her voice, looked at her friend with a new serious look on her face. And as she looked Narinder knew she hadn't been stupid to bring Paula here: because it seemed so much more real, the feel of the danger here in the house, and it was helping her to speak about it – helping her to take the chance to keep hold of her old friend. "I tell you for nothing, Paula, my dad's real scared about something round here, something ... *heavy* ... you know! And it's killing us, Paula, our family ... " And then she could say no more, just because there was no more which she knew to say; and because now, for the first time in front of anyone else, she was crying.

"All right, Nind, all right, mate." Paula was comforting, cuddling her. "Head up, girl – we'll lick it. You've got me – remember?"

And just for that Narinder knew she'd been right to share her mysterious fear.

Leila let herself down from the bus doorway in character, gave no clue to the tough grip she could use, hands and thighs, when she was revving over cross-country bumps on her Kawasaki. Tonight she was a played-out, down-trodden wife, as used to a slapping as a kiss, the sort who thinks equality of the sexes is getting an extra half-hour to do it all in Tesco's. Shuffling along, looking as if she wasn't sure where she was going, she timed her arrival to the second and pushed open the door of Wisener's the Jeweller's just five minutes before closing time.

"Come in, come in, don't let me hurry you, closing up," the shopkeeper told her, "your pleasure is my business."

Leila wandered dispiritedly over to the back of the shop, where Wisener wouldn't pay her too much attention. "Oh, I dunno what to 'ave," she told him. "I dunno what to 'ave to please 'im. I ask you, what sort of 'usband gives you ten quid to go out an' buy your own anniversary present?"

Wisener was still putting things in boxes, standing them ready to go in the safe when he closed the shop. "He must know you have perfect taste, eh?" And he smiled his shopkeeper's smile.

"Oh, I don't blessed know . . . " Leila, eyes on this and that, took the chance to steal a look out of the door. "What do I fancy?" The timing was perfect. Coming across the wide pavement she saw Elkin and Barrett, three grips carried between them and anorak hoods pulled up: anoraks in that Arctic style where the hood comes eight or nine inches forward of the face, shutting it off from icy winds, and from anyone's view. Swiftly, they marched across the last of the pavement and pushed hard into the small shop.

"Your time is my time, my dear," Isaac Wisener was saying, "but I'll just drop the catch on the door."

"You stay where you are!" Leila's voice was suddenly hard and coarse, in her hand was the shine of a pistol, and in an instant Elkin and Barrett were upon the jeweller. Instinctively his hand groped at his panic button.

"You press that button, Isaac, an' I'll 'ave the finger off what done it!" There was no seeing Barrett's face but there were no two ways about his intention.

"Please! I've nothing here," Wisener pleaded. "What will you get for this paltry lot, I ask you?"

But Elkin had thumped the grips on the counter and now he shot his hand over to grab the jeweller's throat. "Wise up, Wisener, you know why we've come!" he told him. "An' I'll tell you, we're having the lot, whether it's sweet Fanny Adams or a fortune! The lot, you hear? Safe, showcases, little shammy bags, all out on the top an' in these, right? Just you leave one ring behind, one ring, an' I'll thread it through your nose!"

And Wisener knew. His face, his shrug, told the others that he knew why they'd come, that the bluff and the defiance had failed. "All right! All right! I don't want so much trouble." Feverishly, and yet reluctantly, delaying those last split seconds before dropping some of the items into the grips, he did what he knew he had to do. He played along now that it was all too late.

"So now you'll know for the future, won't you, Isaac? When you get offered protection you take it, and quick!" Elkin had folded his arms, was watching. "Look at it like insurance, a little monthly outlay, my old son, and nasty things like this don't happen. But you keep saying 'no' and who knows what sort of bad luck you're gonna run into. You do understand, don't you?"

It might have been something precious he was dropping in the grip, or just a huge sense of injustice welling up in him, but Isaac Wisener suddenly aimed a pathetic blow at the man. "You're filth!" he shouted.

Barrett raised a back-hand to hit him, but Elkin was more spiteful than that. "No, son, no!" – and he grabbed the old man's wrist and with two rough wrenches had the rings and the watch he was wearing.

"Please, I'm sorry, not them!" Wisener cried. "They're worthless, I swear to you – sentimental value only ..."

But Elkin's wasn't a heart to be swayed, not by words, not by faces and not by pity. "Sentimental? That's handy, 'cos I'm a sentimental man." He pulled Wisener up onto his toes. "Like, I wouldn't give everyone a second chance, but for you, old son, there won't be no violence. Just so long as when one o' my boys calls in to see you, you pay up like a good 'un! All right?"

"Yes, anything, I promise ... but please, leave me my wedding ring ... An old man's cheap gold ..."

But the personal rings and the watch went flying into the grips.

"We'll have to see." said Elkin. "We'll have to see if you start seeing some sense, won't we?" And he stared at the old man's distress, his smile hidden deep in its hood, where no-one could make out his pleasure.

The shop next to Wisener's at the Boleyn was Patel's the chemist's, where Sam Butler was heading to pick up his tablets. With his cab still dripping from the car wash he drove round out of Upton Lane and squeezed in at an angle at the front of the small parade. He was tired and his actions were slow: but he desperately needed the drug and with his head still held low by the pain he pushed at the cab door. But that was as far as he got. In a sudden blinding flash, with a bright strobe and an almighty ringing, Wisener's burglar alarm went off. Sam twisted his head and stared. Two men with big grips were diving across the pavement towards the Cortina behind him. "No!" he said – and did his very best to look away.

The Cortina doors slammed. The engine revved. A pavement of frozen shoppers waited for the squeal of tyres, like cameras their necks ready to swing with the action. But nothing happened. The car didn't budge, just rocked instead with the sound of angry, muffled voices. And Sam slid sideways in his seat, shut his eyes and waited for the worst.

Ronnie Martin, in the Cortina's driving seat, was desperately trying to fight the automatic control from 'park' into 'drive', cursing the stupid kid who'd stolen a car they couldn't even start with a push.

"Come on!" Elkin's voice cut into the panic. "There y'are! Cab! In that, quick!" He threw a grip to each of the others, grabbed one himself, pulled up his hood and pushed himself out of the get-away car.

From where he was lying sideways in his seat Sam started doing his own cursing as the cab doors slammed and heavy feet scraped in the back. Now he had no option but to sit up.

"Don't look round! Just give it some! An' quick!" It was a voice most cabbies knew: everyone who did business on the streets of the East End recognised an order from Charlie Elkin, although usually he'd be in evening dress or some other social gear. And it froze Sam, there in the strobing light and the ringing.

"You wanna live or what? Move it!"

Not the sort of question Sam needed asking twice. He pushed the cab into gear and pulled away as if he'd been get-away driving all his life, his head bent low and his headache pushed right out of his mind. All he saw was the road clear ahead, all he heard was the clatter of the diesel as the engine struggled to respond: and like a kid in a pedal-car he leant his body into the wheel, urging the vehicle forward, as if his own efforts could somehow make the thing go faster. But just as he was getting up something like a bit of speed, a police car suddenly came screeching out of St. Bernard's Road, cutting across dead in front of him. He threw his body back and stamped the footbrake through the floor.

The cab stopped a foot short and Sam's heart clattered like the diesel. "You stupid berk! For crissake!"

But at least he'd had some warning, had known he was throwing on the brakes. In the back, Elkin and his heavies were just suddenly shot forward, their feet tangled in grips, their arms and hands all over to save themselves. And Elkin, whose hooded face had been crouching and threatening close to Sam's partition, had no chance at all. His head smacked hard into the toughened glass.

"Ow! Blast you!" One hand shot to his fractured glasses the other to the handle on the door. "Come on!" he yelled. "Leave them!" And abandoning the grips he threw the door open, still clutching at the accident inside his hood. But the police were already out of their car, and needing both arms for pumping he let go the fractured frame, lost hold of his lenses, and put his head down to leap out and run blindly off up the road. Barrett and Ronnie Martin leapt out after him, one on either side, and with wild swings at the police as they closed in, the gang took off in two different directions, frightening anyone in their way with the yells they made.

Sam saw them go. As the pain in his head clamped down on him again, he jumped out into the road and watched the villains getting away; then, shaking his head gently, he opened up the back of his cab to see what it was they'd left behind. Three grips, identical, and tucked between two of them, lying there on the floor, something else: half a pair of glasses, broken off at the bridge. Elkin's! Sam blinked, and swore. They had to be, because they hadn't been there an hour ago when he'd cleaned out the inside. Almost without thinking, he scooped them up, rolled them into his driving glove and shoved it in his pocket. The East End way: survival: what you learned in school round there if you wanted to grow up and grow old. And with that vital piece of evidence hot in his pocket Sam sat back in his cab and waited with the patience all cabbies have for the police to come back and for someone senior to take charge.

Detective Inspector Robert McNeill was the man – and he'd have made a powerful villain himself, with his hard Glasgow background and his will to win; but as a youngster he'd learned which way round the world was supposed to spin, and he'd done his best to keep his part of it going in the right direction ever since. People respected him, and above all he respected himself – he knew there were no short cuts in the way he did his job. So he'd been brought down south by one of his bosses and given a brief to root out the likes of Charlie Elkin from London life. Now, big, broad and expensively suited, he stood on the wide pavement at the Boleyn and listened to what forensic had got to tell him.

"Cortina's clean as a whistle, guv, cab's what you'd expect – like fingerprinting the London Underground. And nothing on the floor or down the seats."

McNeill nodded to the man with the silver brush. "Aye." He turned to a woman in plain clothes. "Put the Cortina on the computer, let's have a look-see if these plates are false." The way he held his body said he was aware of the people around him, Wisener the jeweller, Sam the cabbie, people with things to say to him; but the downplay of his hands, his neck, shoulders and his concentrated expression told everyone that he wasn't a man to interrupt. "All right, gi' us out the grips now," he commanded a man in uniform.

Mr Wisener counted them out. "Please God they're heavy," he said as they came out with handkerchiefs slung under their handles.

"Y' understand I'm taking these grips in as evidence?"

"Grips, why shouldn't you? But you don't need my stock and my wedding ring, eh? You won't find any calling cards in there." Wisener's mouth was turned down, his hands turned up. "They weren't beginners, these boys, I can tell you."

McNeill gave the elderly man a full-strength Celtic stare. "Aye, we know that very well, don't we?" He became abrupt, business-like. "You'll have all this back by morning. You can tell your customers it's business as usual."

" 'Usual', he says. What's usual any more?" Wisener asked. "I tell you, this old man's putting the shutters up tonight. For good." And with a slow, bowed, but dignified walk, he crossed the wide pavement and disappeared into his shop.

Sam took his chance, now that McNeill was talking. "Can I get away an' all, guv? You've give my cab the business. They was only in it thirty seconds."

But he might have known it wasn't going to be that quick and easy. McNeill was not a man to be hurried in any direction. "Thirty seconds, did ye say? And how many blinks of the eye is thirty seconds, eh?" he rounded on him. "You know, I find it awfu' hard to credit you didnae see their faces – not even the most fleeting wee glimpse."

But cabbies are used to questions from the police; they definitely don't panic, and Sam had been at the game most of his working life. "That's straight up, guv'nor," he said, almost as if he believed it himself. "I got no more idea who they are than the man in the moon."

McNeill nodded. "Aye," he said, "that figures! An' the same wi' voices, an' all?"

Sam shook his head. "No. London. Cockney, like, normal."

McNeill flapped his notebook shut, didn't bother to write it down.

Sam shrugged his shoulders, the innocent, useless witness. "Be fair, I have got a living to make – and right now you gents are costing me money." He kept his voice flat, just a hint of whine in it, while a tight steel band of pressure seemed to be distorting the shape of his skull.

"Aye, all right, I think we can let you go. Temporarily, you understand."

Sam tapped his cabbie's licence. "Well, you know where I am." And he turned to check the road before getting round to his driver's door – only minutes away now from his bed, closed curtains, two tablets, and the sleep which would take his pain away.

Or he would have been – except for the elderly Sikh woman, laden with stretching plastic bags of food, who crossed the road from the supermarket on the other side and got into the cab before he could stop her.

"Elliott Street, please," she said. "Gurdwara, Sikh temple."

If he hadn't just complained to McNeill that he was losing trade, Sam would have had her out of the cab as quickly as she'd got in, but headache or no he was stuck with this last fare of the day.

"Go on, away," McNeill told him. "An' say a prayer for me while you're there."

The only prayer Sam was likely to say was for himself, though: for his poor old head – and for his life when Elkin found out who the cabbie had been.

The small crowd watched him drive away, their attention taken as a policeman held up traffic to wave him out. Which meant that none of them saw McNeill bend down and pick up something from the gutter: half a pair of glasses which had been shadowed by the cab's back wheel. None of them, that is, except Leila, who, without her wig and her own glasses, and with her coat reversed to show the tartan side out, was standing behind the police tape gawping with the rest, and making some very important mental notes of everything she saw . . .

"Get out the way!"

Anyone coming between Dean and the television when his father wasn't home was likely to get a dose of his playground voice. His sprawling legs took up all the floor and the television sound took up all the air.

"Shut up!" Paula deliberately stood in front of the set to wipe the top of their grandad's musical box with her sleeve.

"*Paula!*"

"You could write your name in this dust – if you could write your name!"

"*Mind out the way!*" Dean shouted.

Paula lifted the heavy inlaid walnut box onto the counter dividing the living room from the kitchen, and gently, with the faintest bell-like ping, she took her hand out from under.

"What you doing now?" Dolly turned down the oven and came over to see. "Did you say dust? Be the day when you lift a duster!" She stroked round a bevel on the box with a tea-towel. "Shows what we breathe in all the time, though, eh?"

Paula raised the musical box's lid, looked into the shining brass and steel interior: the long barrel studded with pins, the slanting steel teeth to engage them, the butterfly wings of the clockwork governor and the angled winding arm – everything oiled and adjusted ready to play when the 'going' lever was pushed. It had been her blind nan's treasure, her treat instead of the telly, and now it was her grandad's pride and joy, his keepsake, which she used to please him by asking for it to be played.

"We can't have that out now," Dolly said. "Your dad'll be in for his tea, and your grandad, when he decides to show up."

Paula closed the lid and carefully carried the heavy instrument back. "Where is Grandad, anyway?" she asked.

"Stayin' out," said Dean, "Hiding 'case you wanna play that thing!"

Paula pulled a ha-ha face. "Who rattled your cage?" But it was odd, she reckoned, Grandad not being here when he'd definitely promised to finish her necklace: not like him at all. She kicked one of Dean's sprawling feet. "You ever switched your eyes off that box you'd know what it was like down the Boleyn. Traffic." And, believing it, she flopped herself in a chair and sat stroking her still bare neck.

Charlie Elkin's place would have taken some sprawling legs to cover. A ranch-style house in the stock-broker belt between Harlow and Chipping Ongar, it had a vast living room where Dolly would have made up sandwiches for going from one end to the other – as large as a film set, with space for cameras and crew and fifty extras. But the only people in it after the raid were Charlie Elkin and Leila Duke, and tonight the feel of well-heeled calm among natural brick and expensive paintings was missing; the electricity in the air, the after-effect of any job, was not of the dry, summer-lightning sort, but thick and thunderous.

Elkin sat on the edge of a wide armchair, his eyes glued to the video'd programme on the television; Leila knelt by the recorder, ready to switch it off when the man gave the word. As the weather man came on Elkin blinked behind his old-fashioned spare glasses and jumped up. "Right, rub that off. Now we seen it they can't say we ain't been here since we left the bingo, watching the box. They can't *prove* we never saw that the right time." He took off the glasses and knuckled his eyes. "Gawd, gives you a headache, though."

Leila pushed the buttons to do as she was told. "Bit of luck you kept those spares, Charlie."

But you had to watch every word with Elkin. He thrust his spares back on to stare at her. "Bit of luck? With my eyes? Give me some credit, woman," he said, "think I'm stupid?" He started pacing round the furniture, breathing in and out noisily as he put himself through some hidden muscle-toning. "You 'ave been on to the optician, 'ave you?"

But Leila had it all in hand. Bright East End girls didn't need any help in taking one logical step after another – even if Leila's life with Elkin did turn her stomach over sometimes in a most exciting way. "Jonesey'll have your new ones round tomorrow. And he said he won't say more than he has to to the Old Bill. But he will have to show them his patients' records – he can't lose yours all of a sudden."

Elkin stopped his pacing and gave her a look. "Oh, no? Then I might have to have a word with Jonesey! They're good as fingerprints, them lenses, with my eyes both different."

Leila sat down, as if she didn't want to seem to be confronting him. "Only if they've got the pair, Charlie. And they haven't, have they? All McNeill picked up was one arm and a lens, and they said the cab was clean. Even he can't get you identified on half a pair of glasses." She dropped her voice, made a suggestion. "Leave it alone, you'll do more harm than good if you lean on anyone now."

Elkin started his pacing again, turning and addressing book cases and paintings wherever he stopped, showing all the uncertainty he could never let the gangs see. He smacked a fist into a palm, a Hollywood gesture he'd seen Bogart do. "That still leaves me sweating on getting that other lens before they do."

"So? We know who's got it, don't we? We know who's got to have it if McNeill's only got the one . . ."

"Yeah. The cabbie." Elkin had stopped to stare at a shotgun mounted on the wall.

"He *must* have it, Charlie. No-one else, is there? It definitely wasn't around, I went over every inch you ran . . ."

Elkin stood and looked at half of Essex through the huge picture window. A man and an Alsatian patrolled on the skyline, but Elkin's, not police. In any case, the law would come up the drive, to the front door in their official cars when they came. He turned back to Leila, suddenly punching his palm again. "Thing is, gettin' at 'im with McNeill breathing down his neck an' mine. It'll be like getting next to royalty."

Leila went over and kissed him, a spark of static in the criminal excitement. "We'll find a way, Charlie. The man's said nothing yet or we wouldn't still be here, would we?"

"Yeah, you're not wrong." They kissed again, and he whispered some of the soft words she wanted to hear. "We'll find the guy's weak spot, some secret, someone he's fond of ..."

"Yeah, Charlie ..."

"Then we'll have him! We'll see how he likes the idea of someone like that getting hurt. Hurt bad. Someone he couldn't stand seein' suffer. Right?"

Leila smiled and snuggled in closer. "Right!" she whispered back. "Be my pleasure, Charlie, that will ..."

three

Saturday mornings are special, if only in a minor way. No-one gets up for school; there isn't that rushing about where every action has to count; there aren't the bangs on the bathroom door; and more often than not there's something to look forward to. For Paula, today, it was the necklace and then a swim, over at Woolwich where they had a wave machine and a crowd of boys who made a few waves of their own. But first – and what got her out of bed early – was seeing how her grandad was feeling after that terrible thing the night before.

No-one was saying too much about that Boleyn hold-up: no-one in the house, anyhow – although all down the street they were at their gates talking about it. But it must have been quite something. To think that her grandad had actually had the crooks in his cab for a few seconds, till he'd been road-blocked and they'd run away. Actually in his cab! Even in the light of day it took your breath away, Paula thought – although with some of the stories him and her dad came home with, not all that hard to believe. At least it had made Dean take his eyes off the telly for five minutes! And no wonder Grandad had gone to bed with one of his headaches. Which made it all the more special of him to want to get her present done, because she definitely wouldn't expect it.

Paula's special present was this delicate necklace in the letters of her name, made from a piece of fine silver Sam had been given instead of a cab fare one night. The decoration and the craftsmanship were superb because, as Dolly often said, her dad could have turned his hand to the finest of metalworking going; out there in his workshop he could easily have spent his days enjoying the quietness of it all; but Sam would never hear of it. "You're left too long with your own thoughts," he'd say, "you brood. . ." And the argument always had to stop there: because there was never any answer to that.

Now Paula leant and watched him buffing the edges on the last 'A' of her name, an intricate little letter in the Roman style with a chased decoration along and around the flat surfaces. She heard him concentrating heavily, holding his breath sometimes as he turned a corner or went into a miniature aperture with a fine file.

"It's beautiful."

The old man chuckled softly. "You can tell who you are in the dark now," he said, running his fingers over the shapes. " 'Paula'. P, A, L, U, A . . ."

"Eh?" Paula's stomach did a turn, but the old man soon started laughing.

"Gawd, you're easier to wind up than your mum!" he told her. And just as quickly his mood changed back, went from laughing to serious all of a sudden, as it often did. "I made something like this for your nan once, bit of gold I had," he told her in a quiet voice, "only with my name on it – Sam, like . . . " Paula watched his face, said nothing, noticed he was carrying on working, still addressing the piece and deliberately not looking at her. "Said it felt funny, she did, written in letters: so I put little braille marks on the back . . . "

"Yeah? That was nice."

"Still keep it round me neck . . . " But he didn't fish for it, just carried on towards the perfection he always wanted. Paula studied him carefully. He hadn't put his hand to his head yet this morning, didn't seem to be having one of his headaches. For a second she wondered whether he might like to tell her about his bad time the night before, now they were on their own – because they did share special things sometimes. But she didn't mention it. If he wanted to, he would, she reckoned; it'd be different, then . . .

He looked up suddenly. "There!" he said. "That shouldn't cut your throat! Now, let's see how it looks."

It was beautiful. As it dangled, fine and intricate, Paula's shoulders shivered with the pleasure of it, feeling her name lovingly worked in silver, a piece of jewellery which no-one else in the world, not even another Paula, could ever go out and buy from the shops.

"Oh, Grandad ..." Sam fastened it, and she pulled a long face as she tried to look down and see it. "I think it's the best present I've ever had."

"It ain't nothing. I've enjoyed making it, girl, kept me out of mischief."

Paula stretched her neck, lifted her chin, started thinking about the clothes that would show the jewellery off.

"Take it off before you go swimming, mind ..."

"I'm not daft, Grandad!" Then she threw her arms round his neck, pulled him over, squeezed him hard. "And I'm over the moon! It's fantastic!"

"Good, so am I." But if she hadn't been so delighted she might have felt the tension in his arms as he returned her hug, might have seen that frown again that was getting to be part of his normal look: due to a headache suddenly starting, or perhaps today due to that something else that was pulling him down.

Paula had decided days before that she definitely wouldn't wear her new necklace swimming, never in a million years. And especially not to the pool where she was going today, where you didn't swim gently up and down the bath like at East Ham or Romford Road, but had ten minutes of waves every half an hour to throw you about and let you surf in – more like a rough seaside than the Olympics. It was over on the other side of the river, on a bus and over the ferry, but it was well worth the effort, and on a Saturday afternoon when Nindy was shut up in her shop, it was a brilliant place to go – and not all that far, not really, not when you thought about the distances country kids had to go for things. A 101 bus to the ferry, over on the boat – she was forbidden the lonely foot tunnel – and you were there.

And the ferry was a breath of fresh air, Paula reckoned. If you spent your week cooped up in a small house there was something great about the wind blowing off the river and ruffling up your hair, standing there staring-out a seagull as it flew alongside, and looking down into the currents where people never came up again, and imagining . . . And it was free: a cockney answer to the Yorkshire Moors or the Broads, and only a bus ride away.

This Saturday, with the beautiful new necklace back home in a padded box, Paula stood on the vehicle deck and looked out over the water. There was always a chill down here, but the sun was shining brightly and the brown water sparkled as if to show off, to pretend it was as good as any other stretch of the river. Upstream, a sugar ship was unloading at Tate's, and the piers of the Thames Barrier seemed to sail silver in the sun. Being weekend, the huge juggernauts which often filled the four lanes of the vehicle deck were absent; in fact the ferry had departed half-full, just a small fleet of cars with a cricket team, a motor-bike and an ice-cream van; so there was an openness, a feeling of space which Paula enjoyed. It really was a little bit like being on your holidays, she thought: and it made her feel sorry for Narinder, indoors in their dark old shop: stuck there all worried about her dad and her mum, instead of being on her way to a swim and a bit of fun over in Woolwich.

The voice, when it spoke, was close to her ear and it really made her jump. "Water looks cold today." Paula spun round. A woman in black leathers and motor-bike gauntlets was leaning on the rail next to her: a good-looking woman with very blonde hair blowing about and a figure you could see through her zipped-up top.

"Yeah, it does."

"Going swimming?"

Paula looked down to her hold-all with its tell-tale sausage of towel sticking out. "Yeah." She tried to make a joke. "But not in there! Over the Woolwich wave-maker."

The woman looked down at the murky water, swirling without its sparkle now in the shadow of the ferry. "You wouldn't last long in there, I don't reckon. Eh, Paula?"

"No ..." Paula's chest suddenly seemed to freeze. "Here, how d'you know...?" *Paula?* Her hand went to her throat: checked that she wasn't wearing the necklace, hadn't kept it on by mistake ... Instinctively, she went to move away – but a firm, gauntleted hand suddenly pressed down hard on one of hers and held her there like an animal with a paw in a trap. "Here, leave off!"

"I know – you've been told not to talk to strangers." The woman's voice was soft and sort of educated, didn't seem to go at all with what she was doing, with the strength pinning Paula there.

"Leggo!" Paula looked round for help, but the cricket team had gone below, the deck was deserted.

"But then, we're not strangers, Paula – at least, you're not a stranger to me."

The woman's eyes were slits in the wind, menacing, and her voice had gone low in her throat, the way a panther might talk. "I know your grandad – well, know of him, and I've got a message I want delivered, that's all." The woman looked around her but she didn't release her grip by a fraction. "Just tell him, the man said to give back what doesn't belong to him. Tell him to ... " And she twisted Paula's head violently with her free hand, hurt her, forced her to look into her thin eyes. "Tell him to stop making waves. Or the swimming could get colder. Tell him that." And with a sudden jerk she grabbed Paula's arm and half-lifted her out over the water. Paula screamed, but in the noise of the wind and the sea-gulls the sound was lost over the wide river. "He'll know what I mean.

Tell him someone who was in and out of his cab yesterday wants to see *eye to eye* with him. Got it?"

"Let go! Let go!" Paula started wriggling and kicking. But the woman wouldn't release her grip.

"I said, *got it?*"

"Yeah, all right!" Paula screamed at her. "I've got it!"

"There's a good girl." And now she did let her go. "And don't you forget! We wouldn't want to overwork the river police, would we?"

She went. With perfect timing she strode back to her parked machine, pulled on her black-visored helmet, straddled her legs, and as the ferry-boat docked she roared up the ramp to Woolwich: while Paula stared after her, her neck hurting, her arm hurting – and her heart thumping with the real fright of what had happened, of the death-threat she'd just had. She watched the big motor-bike get well up into the traffic, and then she turned and went below, stayed on the boat. She was going back. Going home. Any thoughts of water and waves over here where that woman was could only be bad ones right now.

Sam had a biro in his hand when Paula burst into his bedroom. He'd written nothing with it, but he covered up his note-pad all the same.

"Here! Knocking gone out of fashion?"

"Grandad! Sorry, but –" Paula's mouth suddenly felt fixed open. Seeing someone she could tell about it seemed to bring out the scare again, the way a bruise blues in a warm bath. She wanted to cry, but she forced herself on. "I've just had ... someone just tried to ... "

Sam dropped his pen, got up and grabbed her. He knew the look of shock. "You ain't been swimming ... ?" he tried to prompt, feeling her dry hair.

"No ... " Paula was out of breath, she'd run all the way from the bus stop. "On the ferry. Some woman ... all done up in motor-bike leathers ... she threatened me!"

"Do what?"

"Said she knew you, she did ... knew your name, and mine ..."

"Eh?"

"Said something about you ain't got to make no waves ... you gotta give back what don't belong to you ..."

"Oh, yeah ...?" Sam led her over to sit on the bed, his eyes narrowing.

"You gotta see *eye to eye* with some bloke who was in your cab ..." She hoped she'd got it right. But there was no mistaking the next bit. "Or she was gonna push me in the water ..."

"Eh?"

"Held me over, she did. Over the side." Paula rubbed her arm where she could still feel the grip. "She was strong enough to, an' all, I tell you ..."

"Oh, my God!" The old man sat slowly down beside her.

"What's it mean, Grandad? What's it all about? 'Cos I'm scared, really scared, I can tell you!" She stared at his grey face, at the hand that had gone to his head again.

But Sam was saved from answering by another interruption, another development in the same business: someone special to speak to him, announced by Dolly with a quiet knock on his bedroom door.

"Cup of tea downstairs," she told him, coming in. "And a copper. Plain clothes, Mr McNeill, about last night." She seemed to grab a handful of the tension in the room, like picking up washing. "But don't worry, Dad, he hasn't got a ball and chain ..." And seeing Paula looking upset for him, "Nice swim, love?" she asked.

Sam led the way downstairs, while Dolly did a mime for Paula to stay where she was, up there out of the way. Paula pulled a face, but she nodded. She sort of understood: they did it as a matter of course, your mum and dad, tried to keep you out of things – the same way you did them. But that hold-up had something to do with the woman on the ferry, even a kid could work that out, and she was being told to stay out of it when a horrible feeling inside told her she'd already been dragged deeper in. So she wasn't at all reluctant when Dean crept past and beckoned her to the top of the stairs where they could both hear what was going on in the living-room.

Down there, Detective Inspector McNeill was holding his cup of tea with the unmistakeable air of one who wasn't being bought-off by it. He held it out and regarded it suspiciously before each small sip. "Now, hae' I got this right?" he was asking Sam. "You're telling me the man broke his glasses in your cab and ran off wearing just half a pair?"

Sam nodded from the refuge of his armchair. "Something like that," he said – the understood phrase of someone who's telling you he's saying no more than he dare.

McNeill knew the game, the East End's own version of cat and mouse. "But you said you didnae *see* his face." He put down his cup and saucer on the musical box. "Now, did you see it or did you no'?" He squared himself up to Sam, hands in his trouser pockets. "I'm sorry to trouble you, but you c'n understand my wee confusion ..."

Dolly, in the kitchen area, knocked a cup into the sink.

"I *didn't* see it," Sam said, very definitely. "I'm just assuming he ran off with the glasses 'cos there was no way they was in my cab." McNeill said nothing, stood and stared. "They could've caught in his anorak thing, or fell out down the street ..."

"You're saying the glasses broke when you threw on the brakes?"

Sam's hands flew up like two disturbed pigeons and landed back onto the arm-rests. "If you say so, guv'nor. How do I know? I'm driving a cab at the time, remember, being told to put me foot down!"

McNeill shifted his weight, looked as if he were deciding whether to tell Sam the next bit. "There was an arm and a lens in the gutter – dry, not been there long." He paused and stared, held it for a full ten seconds. "So where's the rest? That's what I'm asking myself."

"Search me." But the reply was a bit too sharp, and for a moment McNeill looked as if he just might do that. "I'm sorry I can't be no more help, guv, straight up I am." There was the stare again, from Dolly as well as McNeill, which the policeman broke by walking over to the window nets, looking out, turning back, whistling in his teeth. Then he sat down opposite Sam and blistered a layer of skin off him with his eyes.

"Mr Butler, you're no' impressin' me very much," he said. "I'll tell yae, I've been after a certain wee joker who thinks he runs the East End for five years now. An' this is the closest touch I've come, half a pair of spectacles awa' from nailing him. You jus' gi'es that missing half an' I can tie that villain in wi' armed robbery an' I can send him down for a guid long stretch – plenty o' time to break up his little kingdom." His voice was earnest now, verging on the angry, the cat-and-mouse forgotten for a bit. "But I tell yae, I'm like that prince wi' a glass slipper, I've only got the one and I do need to find the other."

Sam, gripping the chair arms now, stared back at him, set his mouth in a still-saying-nothing line.

The policeman leant further forward still, dropped his voice so that Dolly and the listeners at the top of the stairs had to turn their heads to hear. "But I'll tell you something, my friend. I wouldnae be surprised if I *do* find it, because I will nae stop till I do. And I dinna care whose feet I tread on in the process!"

"Charming," Sam said. McNeill's eyes sharpened. "Prince Charming, the guy with the slipper."

"Aye – and what was the end of the story? Ask yourself that." He got up and threw his shadow over Sam. "They lived happily ever after, eh? Gi' that a wee thought when you're sitting here on your ain ..."

Upstairs, Paula suddenly knew it all. At least, she knew

what the woman on the ferry was reckoning had happened, and she rocked on the top step with the knowledge.

"He's telling pork pies, Grandad is," Dean whispered. "Hear him say 'straight up' just now? He always says 'straight up' when it's something he doesn't mean."

Paula shushed him. "Don't be rotten," she hissed. "How do you know, anyway?"

Dean lowered his voice some more. "I'm not thick! I've heard him. You listen: when he's tired or got a headache he says, 'I feel fine, Doll, straight up.' It's one of his habits. You listen to him."

But Paula knew that she didn't have to. He was right, was Dean: Grandad was definitely hiding something. "He must have some reason, then," she said, very softly. "Poor old Grandad."

At that moment, suddenly and very surprisingly, the living room door opened and McNeill strode into the hallway – and awkward positions and cramped legs stopped Paula and Dean from making any more than the start of a move out of sight.

"Oh aye, what's this?" the detective called up as he saw them. "Wee mice, eh?"

Dean disappeared like a scared rabbit to the safety of his bedroom. But Paula, now that she'd been seen, brazened it out like her mother would and ran down the stairs to cuddle Sam. Deliberately she put herself between him and the big policeman.

"You all right, Grandad? You all right?"

But wee girls showing off didn't bother McNeill. "Oh, I'm sure he is. And I wouldnae be surprised if he won't start seeing things my way before too long." He said it all to Sam's face, not to Paula. "With little sweeties like you to keep from harm, he'll soon see who he oughtae be paying mind to, eh, Sam?" And without saying more, certainly not a goodbye, he opened the front door and went out with a crash. Which left Paula and

Sam staring at one another, neither of them knowing what they could safely say to each other, and Dolly looking pale and sick at the prospect of her old dad being deeper in hot water than he'd wanted her to know.

four

Keeping up the appearances of a normal life in the face of all sorts of investigations was something Charlie Elkin had been used to ever since his first petty stealing at school. He'd learnt then that going missing or doing something out of the ordinary was the quickest way of drawing everyone's attention: so he'd always kept up all his normal ways, mucked about in class even when his pockets were stuffed with tapes from the teachers' cars. And now, in the middle of all this business, Sunday came and it was his muck-about day, so being an indulgent man, and astute, he did Leila's moto-cross thing with her.

Not that he really mucked about at it: it was a very professional session, with Elkin shouting advice and keeping very strict timings as she tried to shave seconds off her best. He had his own little wood at the side of his property, a triangle of trees with ups and downs and plenty of overgrown clumps, an ideal spot for private practice, and that's where Leila perfected her brave skills – where she forced herself to keep throttling on going down when other people would have braked, to throttle back at the crest where others would roar into the air and lose seconds, to push her machine over at angles which sometimes defied gravity.

But this Sunday the practice had another purpose. Elkin, in a new pair of glasses, Jones's rushed-job replica of the ones he'd lost, was clinging-on behind her on the big Kawasaki, bouncing up and down like a kid, making sure the tyre-marks in the mud were deep enough for two-up. They came to a stop at the top of a rise and Elkin got off in a flap of trench-coat.

"How was that?" Leila asked.

"I had to hold 'em tight. Anyone can get their glasses shook off an' ruined, a sport like this."

"What a rotten shame."

"An' we've been *miles*, 'aven't we?"

"*Miles*!" She laughed. "They could be anywhere in all that undergrowth."

"Yeah," he said. "Water-tight, unless he gets the other lens. Right eye's two-a-penny, but it's this left one, not matching it, that's what makes 'em mine." He took his new glasses off, looked through them, as if to prove his point, and as he put them back his expression changed, like donning a mask, from talking about his own weakness to suddenly turning hard.

"You wasn't too soft with that kid, was you? Too subtle? You did spell it out for her, what we'd do?"

Leila revved her bike, loudly. "I only held her out over the water!" she said, letting the sound die. "She got the message all right!"

"Yeah ..." Elkin walked about, spun, kicked at some bushes. "Still, all the same, I think I'm gonna have a word with the old man. Myself. Think I'll make things crystal clear for the old idiot!"

"Easy done, Charlie – but I thought you wanted to stay clear."

"Well, I've changed my mind." His voice rang loud round the trees. "An' I want their place gone through, turned right over. He's got them bins somewhere, I know he has."

Leila wriggled on her saddle, leaned forward, looked anxious to go again. "But you said ..."

"Right!" Charlie's shout sent up a couple of birds the motor-bike hadn't flushed. "It'll put him straight, that will, if I get in right under the nose of McNeill!" He rounded on Leila, gripped her shoulder hard. "I do want this settled, you hear? I don't want it hanging over me, I want to be able to sleep easy again."

"All right, Charlie, I'll set it up. No sweat, love." Leila

revved again. "Now come on, we came out for a bit of sport as well. You going to time this one?"

Elkin, buoyed up by her confidence, suddenly relaxed. "Time it?" he asked, nodding at the up and down terrain, "Gawd, I could run it quicker'n you can ride it."

"Oh, yeah?"

"Yeah! Easy! No-one beats Charlie Elkin, I tell you, not on his own patch. And I mean *no-one!*" He slung off his trench-coat and tossed it onto a bush. Underneath, he was track-suited, ready for action.

"You gonna say it, then?" Leila called, crouching ready.

"Yeah, I'll say it," he shouted, leaning forward. "Kill!" And with a John Wayne wave of his arm he spurted off down the track, taking Leila's line and forcing her to bump on the verges: showing from the off that on his own patch no-one ever put anything over Charlie Elkin.

Elkin's adversary, Sam, was lying on his bed and staring at the fancy coving on the ceiling. It was that sort of time, on a Sunday evening, when the light begins to fade and, after a lie-down, you have to make the effort to splash your face and do something with the few hours left. Unless you're depressed, when the effort seems too big to make, and you go on lying and imagining, reality and fantasy melting at the edges, till you're no longer sure whether you're sixty, or twenty-six or sixteen. You lose yourself for dozes at a time, and people come and talk to you, things happen, which seem so real that even after you've come-to they take a time to fade.

"Can I come in?"

"Eh? Yes, mate, come on ..." Sam couldn't remember how much he'd told Nell about this latest rotten business, the headaches seemed to put him off his stroke so much; but she'd understand, he knew; she always had ...

"Grandad, you all right?"

Grandad? The old man sat up so quickly his head went light.

44

He'd been years away. "Good God! I thought ... Come in."
He rubbed his eyes, tried to look a bit here-and-now.

"'Ave you got a minute?"

"'Course! I've got all the time in the world for you, love.
Come in and shove the wood in the hole." His face said he felt a
bit of a fool, and his voice came out a bit too jolly.

Paula shut the door quietly behind her, stood with her back
to it to prevent anyone bursting in. "Grandad ..." She wasn't
sure how to begin. "It's about them glasses ..."

"Oh, hello, Big Ears." Sam spoke as quietly as she had.

"I wasn't meaning to listen –" Paula started lying; then she
thought better of it. "Well, I was – and I did hear what that
policeman was saying."

Sam leant forward, his elbows on his knees: "About that
crook? Love, 'ave you got any idea who that joker is?"

"No ..."

"Not his name, I don't mean. I mean, do you know how big
he is?" He was staring her in the eyes, was trying to impress
her. "He's the biggest crook in town. He's so big he's got the
whole of the East End eating out of his hand. They're like a
load of pigeons in Trafalgar Square, all up his arm, queueing
up to eat."

Paula snorted. "About time one of 'em done something on
his head, then!" She came away from the door; she seemed to
be getting to say what she wanted a bit quicker than she'd
thought she would.

"Yeah, be nice, wouldn't it?" Sam got up and looked out at
the dusk. "Everyone thinks like that sometimes – but no-one's
got the guts to do it, girl. Not with him." He came back to her.
"An' I'm sorry to tell you, but that goes for your old grandad
an' all." He squeezed her, kissed her on the forehead. "Specially when he starts threatening my family ..."

But Paula wasn't in the mood to take that. She'd been
stewing over all this too long to let a kiss and a squeeze be the
end of it. "Hold on. If the police get the rest of them glasses,

they've got him, haven't they? That's what that C.I.D. was saying. He'll get put inside for years …"

"So they reckon!" Sam gripped the girl's arm. "And where do you reckon one of us'll get put? Fancy being fished out of Barking Creek one dark night, do you?"

"No! They wouldn't!" Her voice sounded disbelieving: but the thought of what that woman had done to her on the ferry was hard to shake.

"They would. That's the sort they are, I tell you …"

Paula fell silent, and for a few seconds they just stared at one another, still wearing their scared expressions: which made her next question sound all the more direct and out of the blue. "Grandad, *have* you got them glasses?" she asked him softly.

Downstairs a doorbell rang but neither of them seemed to hear it. Sam didn't say a word; didn't nod his head, didn't shake it; he just looked at her the way a parent looks when a toddler first asks where babies come from. And then Paula knew for certain. That ferry thing definitely hadn't been some weirdo, and Grandad going into his shell wasn't just his headaches. He was all caught up between big crooks and the police, and the poor old devil didn't know how to get himself out of it.

But she did. "Let me take them glasses in. We can do it somehow, eh?" She was suddenly tugging at his sleeve, the way she'd done when she was little. "You can't just … let him frighten us, get away with everything, not if you've got them glasses." Sam didn't look swayed. "It's like at school: if you don't tell on the bullies nothing gets stopped. They're always telling us that."

But the old man was shaking his head; not so much in disagreement as in sadness. "I know what you mean, mate," he said, "but this ain't a *bit* like school. We're talking about the real big boys now: the big boys in the big bad world." And as if to emphasise what he was saying the door bell rang again, and went on ringing: because the thumb on the button was leaning, hard.

46

Paula had sometimes wondered how she'd cope in an emergency: whether she'd panic if the fire-bell rang for real, what she'd do if they saw a kid fall in the river – and how brave she'd be if the man at the door had come to push in and rob them. Now she was going to find out: because the ringing at the bell was Barrett and Ronnie Martin come to turn the place over, and she was going to feel the fear for the others, the blood-in-the-mouth anger, and the tight frustration of being a victim. And in circumstances like that, she found out, you don't get the chance to cope at all. What she remembered most, weeks afterwards, was the sudden, violent shouting as it started to happen, the dull thumps against the walls, the feeling of it all being some nightmare – and the terrible state at the end of it.

Her dad must have opened the door because she heard his shout, then her mum screamed and Dean shouted, going berserk. Next there were these frightening feet racing up the stairs and Sam's door was suddenly thrown open. Even up till then, for some weird reason, she'd got it in her mind that these were police. But what came round the door was a balaclava: and no police carried knives.

"We pulled the phone out – an' we ain't gonna be long. Behave yourselves, don' let's 'ave no heroes, an' you'll be all right. But one stupid move an' I'll get violent – right?" The man waved the knife close – so close he couldn't have cared all that much.

"Paula!" It was her dad from downstairs, but his voice was quickly muffled off.

"She's O.K!" Sam shouted, but he got his head pushed hard against the wall; and he stood and hugged Paula close to him, didn't make any move to get them hurt, just had to watch the raider go about his rotten business.

And he was very thorough, he didn't leave anything to chance. He'd done all this before, that was for certain. While the same sounds of searching came up at them from the rest of the house and out in the shed, this man turned Sam's room upside down and inside out. Furniture went over and the carpet came up, floorboards were lifted where there were any signs of splintering. Lamp fittings, the mattress, the wardrobe and the boarded-up fireplace, nowhere was missed in the twenty minutes of sweating and swearing. Because this was no stage search, no giving a fright and making a mess to teach them a lesson. This search was for real, Paula could tell, the pressure was on for finding those glasses.

There were more of them upstairs as well, not just the man in Sam's room; she could hear the lavatory chain being pulled, the bath panel crashing off, glass getting smashed in the other bedrooms. And then just as suddenly as it had all started, it stopped, and with another fierce warning to keep on keeping quiet, her grandad was grabbed by the arm and taken downstairs, and Paula was told to follow. "An' don' be stupid or the ol' fool gets it!" she was warned.

Paula could have cried, could have shouted in that anger and frustration when they shoved her into the living room. Four other men in balaclavas were in there, empty-handed. And there against a wall stood her dad and her mum, with a tall and dead-eyed man gripping Dean in a dog's hold. The room looked as if a cyclone had lashed and torn its way around it. The aquarium still slurped dirty where they'd raked under the gravel, the television and the musical box were tipped over on their sides, the kitchen was a clutter of broken plates and turned-out cupboards. And all the family could do was just stare at one another in their terrible state of shock.

"You bleedin' *toe-rags*!" Sam shouted. "I could've told you you was wasting your time if you'd asked! Just look at this!"

"Shut up, Grandad! We ain't done with you yet!" one of the masked men shouted back, pushing him. "Anyhow, not much got broke – she c'n soon clear this lot up."

"You'll leave him be!" Mick rushed forward at the man;

but he didn't get two paces before one of the others had him round the neck.

"Behave yourself! He's goin' outside for a word with the man – an' no-one's gonna stop him."

"Dad!" Dolly made a move for her father, but there were hands to hold her back as well. "You harm one hair of his head and I'll kill you!"

"Oh, do leave off!" The tall man tightened his grip on Mick. "Can't you keep her in order? Five minutes, he'll be, that's all – but one of you so much as burp an' he *will* get hurt!"

So they hustled Sam out, while Dolly and Paula, shaking and sobbing, made a first pathetic attempt to tidy the room just to keep their hands busy.

Sam wouldn't have had to be a mind-reader to know who was out there in the car; not when he knew who'd been in the Boleyn robbery. Forcing him to this meeting had only been a question of time, given what McNeill had found. What no mind-reader would have known, though, what he could only have imagined, was the cold feeling of violence the man gave off, sitting next to him in the back of a big Mercedes. Sam was well used to the famous – few London cabbies don't get a TV star every so often – but this close presence was something very different. It was like being pushed into a car next to an evil force.

Elkin made a pretence at being human. "Sorry about that in there – but you do know the game, Sam, don't you?"

"No, I don't; straight up, I don't. I'm still waitin' for someone to tell me." Sam's voice was thin, the words sounded hard to get the tongue round – but he wasn't going under without a fight.

"Come on! You 'ad word, through the girl. You know what I'm after."

"Yeah?" Now it was all innocence: a game both of them

knew. Bargaining – if you had something to bargain with – usually had to start this way.

But Elkin seemed to think he could ride rough-shod over all that. In a grab he tore his glasses off his face and thrust them at Sam. "I want my other bins back! An' quick! I know the filth was here yesterday, an' I know what he was saying." He put his glasses on again, suddenly dropped his voice to sound more reasonable. "An' I'm not stupid, Sam. He's got half of 'em and he wants you to give 'im the rest."

The old man sat silent. There was even room in the back of the big car for him to lean forward and rest his elbows on his knees: he seemed to be giving the business some thought, until he sat back again and turned to face Elkin – and in the calmest voice going he started taking a very brave line.

"You know something, Mr Elkin, you've just made a big mistake, talking like than, an' turning my place over, showing yourself. 'Cos you've left me knowing too much now." Elkin was staring at him, frowning. "I could stand up in court an' finger you for that – which leaves me feeling about as cosy as a tortoise out of its shell . . . "

"Do what?" It sounded as if Elkin couldn't believe his ears. No-one ever dared to face him out like this.

"See, even if you got your glasses back, I couldn't feel safe, could I? Get me out the way then an' you're laughing, aren't you?"

"Listen, *old man* . . . !"

"But on the other hand, all the time I know where they are, then *I'm* laughing, aren't I? Because if anything sudden did happen to me, or my Paula, or the boy – then, bingo! Up they come, your specs, smack into Mr McNeill's sweaty hands." Sam sat back, wringing his own hands clammy, with a shaking going on which almost rocked the car. Because what he'd just said, if he'd got it wrong, was suicide talk, death-warrant stuff.

But Elkin was suddenly laughing, "Oh, do leave it out,

Grandad, you're jokin' – we could sort the lot of you, tonight, right now." He snapped his muscular fingers.

"*And they'd still turn up, Mr Elkin.*" Sam's voice was quiet and deadly earnest. "That is the point I'm tryin' to make. I've left word ..."

As quickly as it had come, the laughing stopped, the smile disappeared. "So what you saying, then? Exactly?"

Now Sam pushed the bluff, even started to make a move. This was the terrible moment when he'd find out if it had worked. "I'm saying that I've hid them, Mr Elkin, somewhere where you wouldn't find them if you broke up a million houses. So all you've got to do is leave me and my family alone. Make sure I die natural, when my time comes. That way they stay hid – nothing ever gets found, you got my word on that: but you lift a violent finger an' – bingo!" He did a conjurer's flourish with his shaking hands; and with Elkin staring at him, slid along the seat, pushed the handle, and quietly clicked the expensive door. For a few tense seconds he didn't move – and then the miracle happened. His old legs somehow took him in a straight line to the house: and Elkin stayed put: and no-one raised another hand against him.

five

Narinder couldn't remember when she'd last had a laugh.
Well, she could, it had been one of those aching, croak-in-the-
throat things which left you weak, after Scott had cut out a
shape in metalwork – meant to be a circle but had turned out
looking like a sausage. The dance he'd done with that! But that
seemed to have happened in some other world. Everyone had
grim, solemn, scared faces round here nowadays. Where her
dad used to skip her along the pavement to the gurdwara, now
he took the car – and took as much time looking in the
rear-view mirror as he did at the road ahead. Where her mum
used to talk to her, laugh with her, tell her little things not
meant for her dad, now she only ever seemed to answer direct
questions, and then with ratty questions of her own.

At first she'd thought that was what growing up was like: it
was natural. Someone at school had gone on about parents
becoming different people when you get in your teens: the
'awkward age' being theirs more than yours. But she'd soon
realised that wasn't it – not once her dad started turning the
television down to hear sounds around the place; asked who
was in there when the bathroom door was locked; and booked
everybody in and out of the building like soldiers in a barracks.
It was fear, a running scared from something that was changing their lives, and a crazy, unhappy existence it was. All right,
Narinder knew it had never been easy being a Sikh family
living in Shepherd's Gate, it was never as relaxed as liberal
whites liked to think, but it had never been as tense as this
before, not round these streets. Because what her mum and
dad seemed to be frightened of wasn't dog's muck through the
letter-box any more, but petrol every time, and she didn't

know the first thing about helping them cope with that. All she could do was sadly see them change, bite her tongue when she wanted to shout, and help with the ordinary headaches of business by giving a bit more of a hand.

On the Monday, after school – a day when Paula must have had a pain she was that quiet – Narinder hurried home and counted supermarket leaflets into quires, wrapping up the finished bundles in off-cuts and sealing them round with brown tape. But it wasn't the way it had used to be, fun to help, standing alongside her dad and feeling grown-up and proud. Now he had that anxious look on his face, kept stroking down his beard with both hands at once – a sure sign of edgy words to come – and kept throwing an eye over at the door. At one point Narinder stacked a bundle on top of another, let it get a bit off-balance and had to be quick to catch them as they fell.

"Be careful, if you're going to help."

A month ago he'd have said, "Well caught!" – made for the phone to ring the test selectors.

But at that moment the only ringing was a sudden call from the shop door, and Narinder thought her father would leap up onto the work-top, he jumped so high. He left the press running and sidled cautiously round the counter till he could see who it was. With more nervous stroking he shouted to Narinder above the clack of the machine.

"Go upstairs. I want to see this man on my own." No 'please', no 'Nindy'. Just the bare bones, and "Hurry up, then!"

Narinder went, as Pratap pulled the plug on the machine. She ran up the open wooden stairs to the living accommodation and slammed the door at the top. Let him hear her hurry, the pathetic, frightened man! But what she knew about this door was that when you banged it hard like that it always bounced open again – and with her mother making noises in the kitchen she reckoned she could lie up there and listen.

Because if she didn't somehow find out what all this business was about she was going to explode, she knew she was.

The man who came in was youngish and wearing a suit. He could have been selling supplies, except for the slow swagger, the rolling shoulders of a bloke who fancied himself as a bit on the tough side. And if Narinder had been outside Oakwood Underground on the Friday, she'd have recognised the man who'd stolen the Cortina, the get-away driver who'd sat so long outside East Ham market.

"What's up, Squire? You don't look too pleased to see me," he smirked at her father.

She could hear the higher tone of Pratap's nervousness. "Could that possibly be because I'm not?"

The man laughed at her father as he inspected this and that on the work-top. "Come on, two weeks is two weeks, my son. Even you lot can work out two weeks, can't you?"

Narinder had to fight herself to keep still. She'd never learned how not to get angry at that sort of remark, especially made to someone as gentle and intelligent as her father. She wanted to scratch down their racist faces.

"Oh, I can work out two weeks, thank you," her father was saying. "What I cannot work out is why I should pay any more money to you at all."

From the top of the stairs Narinder saw the white yob pick at a spot. "Look, sunshine," he folded his arms, "we explained all that before, didn't we? How London's full o' people who don' like your sort – Gawd, don' you read the papers or nothing?"

Pratap kept his mouth shut: and with a huge effort to keep lying on her angry, rolling stomach, Narinder somehow didn't shout out either. It was obvious her father had some good reason for keeping his cool with this person.

"It's easy, friend. You pay us an' we give you protection; we make sure nothing *nasty* happens to you." He waved his arm at the stairs. "Got kiddies, 'ave you? Like I said, sounds like a good deal to me when you've got kiddies."

Narinder wriggled back, narrowed her eyes. So that was it, then! That was why Pratap Singh was keeping quiet under all this and hadn't gone for his kirpan to drive the filth out on its sharp point. He was scared for her. For Narinder. They'd got the father where it always hurt.

"See, my guv'nor does hate to see kiddies having accidents – 'specially when they can be avoided. Now, hundred quid a month's very reasonable, he reckons, to make sure the kiddies don't get hurt. Or don't you reckon that? I got it wrong, 'ave I, don' your people love their kids like we do?"

There it was again. The racist bit. Trying to wind people up by pretending their feelings couldn't be the same as yours. But her father wasn't letting him get away with it, not altogether. "Now you do surprise me!" he was saying, leaning over the work-top towards the man. "You know, I had never thought to hear a word like 'love' come out of a mouth like yours." But Narinder knew that he'd made a mistake. It never did to stoop to their own level of insult, especially when they only wanted an excuse – because all the man did was pick up a litre bottle of black stamping ink from the counter, unscrew the top, and tip it out in thick pulses all over the floor.

Pratap shouted, made a move for the man round the counter, but the ink had quickly made a barrier between them.

"Oh, dear, now look what I've gone and done! Don't walk in that, Chief, or you'll leave black footprints all over the shop!"

For a hateful second Narinder wanted to fly out, rush downstairs and tear her hands at his face; but something held her there; and it wasn't fear, but some sort of wisdom, that had come.

"So what's the answer then, Squire? What do I go an' tell Mr Elkin?" He had another bottle in his inky hand, its cap off, was menacing all the leaflets Narinder hadn't wrapped – all the profit gone, and most of the costs, if he ruined them.

"Put down that bottle, please."

"What you say, then?"

Pratap's hands fell to his sides. He took in a long, inward-sighing breath which seemed to suck in all the defeat hanging in the room. "Tell him, all right," he said. "But I must have time to pay. Business is very bad just now."

The bottle was put down on the work-top. The man was smiling. "You've made a good decision, shown a little bit of sense, my son. Mr Elkin'll be well pleased with you." And he turned to go.

Narinder watched him, watched her father watching him. He wasn't out of the shop yet, and he'd have to have his last vicious little word she knew.

He had it with his elbow. As he went he elbowed the open bottle he'd just set down, and another glistening pool of black spread across the work-top and ran down its sides to the floor.

"Oh, dear! Clumsy ol' me! Sorry, son." The man swaggered back to the door. "See you in a coupl'a weeks, eh?" And the slam seemed to make even the heavy press jump.

Pratap stood rigid and stared at the slowing drips. What use was action, were cloths, his tension said, when he had to get hold of his rage.

But Narinder had boiled over. "You can't let him do that!" she shrieked from the top of the stairs. "The police! Get on the phone to the police!"

But her father didn't move: except his mouth, and hardly even that. "No. That would be a mistake." She could hardly hear him. "This time it's only ink that's dripping on the floor."

"What else you gonna do, then?" Narinder's voice would do for the two, for two hundred of them.

"Clean up the mess to begin with." Suddenly relaxing, he started throwing sheets of scrap onto the setting ink.

"Yeah, but Dad! You're giving in!" She came clattering down the stairs.

He stopped the throwing and turned to face her, his eyes full with tears: full, and then suddenly overflowing. "No, I'm not giving in, Nindy, I'm getting out. Quick as I can fix it – back to Jullundur."

And in that awful instant Narinder was overcome with a nausea much worse than feeling sick, a falling away of her inside like the worst fairground rides: because she had seen the humiliation, she had heard the hatred and she had felt the fear: and suddenly, now, she knew the words. If he meant what he had said then her life, as she had known it, was coming to an end.

Paula, coming home from school, had had a shock of her own: not like the terror of her house being searched, nor like Narinder's upset, but a nasty shock, all the same. As she'd rounded the corner, hurrying to check that nothing else had happened during the day, she'd suddenly been faced with the sight of her grandfather being led across the pavement to her dad's taxi. And not the grandad she knew, either, but someone who'd suddenly moved on from being a busy cabbie into a frail old man. Perhaps it was the slippers, or the bent-over head. Perhaps it was the way he was gripping his musical box tight, with the not-belonging look old people have; but whatever it was, it was pathetic, her dad leading him across the pavement to the black cab, her mum following up with a small suitcase.

"Grandad! Where you going? Round the doctor's?" But she knew it wasn't that: this looked like hospital.

"Yeah, I'm gonna give him a tune!" Sam said, with a real try at a smile.

"Grandad!" Paula stood in his way.

"I'm all right, girl. I'm going to Frank's for a couple of weeks, that's all."

Dolly put an arm round the old man. "They've got a good doctor over Uncle Frank's – and Auntie Ellie doesn't have to go to work all day. I want the old chancer kept an eye on."

Paula stared into Sam's watery blue eyes. *And* the other reason! her look tried to say: but how could Ilford ever be far enough away? It wouldn't make a scrap of difference to Elkin or that McNeill. "I don't want him to go," she said. She followed him into the cab. "Grandad, I don't want you to go!"

Ever since her gran had died her grandad had lived in their house. All right, it had meant he'd had her bedroom all this time, and she was still in a partitioned room with Dean. But having him go now, seeing him off to Auntie Ellie's just when he needed looking after, that was all wrong: that was cruel.

"I'll be all right, girl. See their doctor, get on me feet again. It's only for a week or two." He winked at her, but even doing that seemed to hurt him. "Keep your mum happy, eh?"

But Paula couldn't see it. If everyone wanted it, her mum could stay at home and look after Grandad, couldn't she? After all, it was Uncle Frank she worked for, her own brother in his car showroom; couldn't he give her the time off? At least she was Grandad's own daughter: better than old Auntie Ellie swanning around, only pretending to feel sorry for him. No, there was definitely some other reason for all this.

"It's those men, Grandad. You're trying to hide, aren't you? It's not the doctor at all."

Sam's hand went to his forehead. "Oh, it is, mate, it is. Now you forget those men. That stuff's all over and done with. Finished. Straight up, it is."

"Grandad!" Paula chided.

"All right, listen, the man knows. I've told him straight. Anything happens to me an' someone'll do the business with the copper." He was keeping his own voice down while Mick and Dolly hovered outside with a neighbour. "I wasn't going to tell you just yet."

"Who will? Who'll do the business?" Paula said it urgently. This could be life and death, and they were all in it now, weren't they?

"You'll find out. I've left word, don't you worry. No-one won't know, 'less something nasty, like ... happens ... then word'll get out where the rest o' them bins is. Take you straight to 'em."

Paula frowned. "But won't it take Elkin an' all?"

"Code, girl. In code, it is. It's all worked out, love, so don't you worry. Anyhow," the old man patted her hand, "it ain't gonna happen. We understand each other, him an' me."

"But a code's got to be *cracked*." Paula pursued it. She still didn't get how his mind was working. "Who's got the ... like, the key?"

Her voice had risen. "Sshh!" he told her. He looked out of the cab window: then he gripped her with his eyes. "You. You'll have the key, girl. If need be."

"Me? What d'you mean? How, Grandad?" From the way he was talking it sounded as if she was still the only one who really knew what he was up to: as if he was trusting her in front of her mum and dad ... Paula swallowed. Was it just because she knew more than them? God! It made her feel proud, whatever reason – but what a load to carry! It turned her stomach over. She knew how these things worked after that business on the ferry – and then the way the house had been searched ... He'd been right, these were the real big boys, these... She opened her mouth to say something, although she didn't know what: a thank you for the trust, or just 'I'm scared!' But before she could get a sound out, her mother put her head in and cut the moment dead.

"You comfy, Dad? Want a blanket?"

Sam snorted – and that seemed to hurt him, too. "What d'you think I am, a bloomin' racehorse?" Then, to Paula, quietly. "I'll let you know, don't you worry. I'll be in touch."

"No, I will, Grandad. I'll come and see you, soon, tomorrow ..."

"Be nice..." He gave her a kiss on the cheek. "But I'm gonna be right as ninepence, love, *an' so's everything else*. You stop worrying, all right?"

"Yeah. All right."

But it was a brave smile and a very shaky wave that saw the cab pull away down the street towards the Barking Road. Paula cried. It was like the end of a phase of her life, seeing her grandad go. And with that sadness – even though she tried to kid herself out of it with a sniff and a rub of her eyes – came a hollow, ominous feeling that she wouldn't be very happy about what was going to happen next.

Dolly's brother, Paula's Uncle Frank, was the one who'd made it good: he was the East End boy who'd started without money or an influential background but with the good fortune to have inherited his father's talent for engineering and a certain business sense. So he'd left school early and gone into a garage, doing up old cars on the side and selling them at a profit while he was learning his trade. The year he was twenty, after a particularly good month at the kerbside, he'd taken a chance and rented a yard of his own: which had soon led to a lock-up, then a side-street lot, and finally to a main-road showroom where he gradually built up a reputation for selling high quality used cars. From being nobody his good name became something he could scarcely afford to lose. Every vehicle with 'Frank Butler Motors' on it was guaranteed neither to be cheap nor a let-down. Those who wanted a bit of style started going to him; the better 'chauffer-driven' hire firms used him; the film world sometimes set him searching for a particular model in good order; and those with a love of fine tuning or walnut and leather always knew who to see: eventually a used 'Frank Butler' became as good a status symbol as something new. All of which had taken him away from the narrow streets where his sister and his father lived and out to the drives and the cul-de-sacs of Ilford: all right, not as far out as the Chipping Ongars of a Charlie Elkin – hard work never brings the same rewards as family wealth or crime – but far enough out to be posh. All of which Auntie Ellie loved. While Frank would have secretly been just as happy living above the showroom back at

East Ham, close to the cars he loved, Eleanor enjoyed the airs and the social activities of a less hand-to-mouth life, and her lips and vowels had quickly tightened to adapt to it. For as long as Paula could remember she'd given the children Christmas *boxes* instead of presents, she always ate Sunday lunch instead of dinner (even in the evening), and in artificial light she'd been known to pretend to have trouble telling fivers from fifties. In her house, hardship meant running low on Martini, and the breadline was a place in the freezer above which Frank was discouraged from storing sliced loaves. And this was where Sam was going – for the benefit of the improved medicine the healthier enjoy: to a bedroom next to his grown-up grandson, Brian, and a chair in the lounge with a view of the pergola.

Mick's cab pulled up outside *Twin Trees*. A car stood in the driveway, but Mick parked across the access all the same, just to annoy. Loudly, he sounded the horn. "That'll get her out of her hammock!"

But Ellie must have been watching for their arrival because already she was coming from the front door, arms open wide like an actress at the final curtain. "You've brought him, then," she called. "Lovely."

Dolly got out of the cab and the sisters-in-law kissed cheeks without actually touching. Ellie leaned into the back. "Hello, Dad. Welcome to Ilford, eh?"

It was a time of bright smiles, everything being made light of, except the old man's big case which Mick had had up the front.

"Here, what you got in here, Dad, all my best silver?"

"Be light if I did have, Mick!" Still clutching his precious musical box Sam bent himself out of the cab.

"Leave that case, Mick. I'll call Brian – he's just come in," Ellie commanded.

Dolly gave Mick a sideways look. As secretary to her brother she knew how little time Brian spent on his father's business. Where he got to half the time was one of the biggest topics of conversation out of Frank's hearing.

"Bri-an!" It was like the call of a teacher, refined and effective at the same time: and Brian appeared on cue in the house doorway.

"Hello, Grandad, Uncle Mick." With the dutiful smile of a good grandson and nephew, the young executive came forward and stretched his hand out for the big case. "Here, I'll take that."

Mick looked down at the hand and gave it a comedian's stare. "Hello! What's this? You havin' a change of colour, Bri?"

Dolly and Sam both looked at the young man's hand, at its staining of black printer's ink.

"What? Do me a favour! No, something got spilt, that's all."

"Oh, yeah?" And the slow family procession walked up the slope of the drive and into the house; where, over weak tea and one biscuit each, Sam was handed over, and Brian went back to the bottle of bleach in his bedroom.

Leila Duke had seen the old man off from East Ham, too, had seen Paula's tears and had followed the cab to Ilford at a safe distance: on her large motor-cycle had stayed to see the patient and his luggage being taken into the house by Brian before her wheels had burned the road in acceleration to report to Charlie Elkin what she'd seen.

He was in his large garden swimming pool – and given her news that warm afternoon it might as well have been filled with champagne.

"Sam Butler's gone to his son's at Ilford. Frank's. Suitcases, all the etceteras, packed up and gone."

Elkin hardly responded: looked at her with one 'Moby Dick' eye as he turned to swim another easy length.

"Think about it, Charlie! Frank! Frank Butler's! Out at Ilford . . ."

The swimmer stood up. Water ran off him like threats. Eyelashes bunched, he had a starry-eyed look. "Frank Butler ... *Butler*. Not Bri Butler's old man?"

"That's the one!"

"Gordon Bennett!"

Leila unzipped her leather top and threw it onto a plastic chair. "Didn't ring a bell with me, neither. But don't you *see*?"

"Yeah! Yeah, I do." Elkin suddenly arched himself backwards under the water again and came up making Tarzan noises. "Just what the doctor ordered! Gawd, we've got the old devil now! We're inside, Leila-girl, inside!" He spumed up a fountain, bubbly, sparkling: the happiest he'd been since losing his glasses on the raid. "Oh, come on in, girl, the water's beautiful!" And with a long strong, slippery arm he grabbed her, and without dreaming of saying no, nor wanting to, Leila let herself be pulled into the celebration with him.

"He spilt ink all over the floor, for the purpose." Narinder stopped shaping her copper tea-spoon to go on with her story. "And my dad didn't do anything – 'cept saying about India."

Paula stopped too. It was usually a good place to talk, the metalwork classroom, last thing in the afternoon, with all the rasping and banging going on; but beating copper today wasn't quite so handy: there was a great tendency for everyone to stop hammering at once.

"Nind! He can't do that!"

"No? You tell him, then!"

"Nind, you can't go."

Narinder looked up from her spoon and stared at her old friend. It had finally got through to her after telling her all day: that she was definitely going away and never coming back.

Paula lifted an arm as if she suddenly wanted to hug her.

But, "What you makin', Prescott? A frying pan?" Tommy Parsons was having a wander round the class.

"No! Keep thinking it's your head an' can't stop hitting it!"

But when she turned back the chance for a bit of comfort had gone. Paula picked up her spoon and looked at it. It *was* a bit flat and big for a teaspoon: all the tea-leaves would fall off. Narinder's on the other hand, was beautiful: well-shaped and nicely beaten to a smooth sheen.

"I wanted this for my grandad," Paula moaned; "but he'd feel so ashamed of me ..." She fingered the delicate necklace she wore hidden under her uniform. Tonight they were going over to Ilford. "He'd make his headache worse, laughing ..." She threw it down among the scraps on the bench.

"Why don't you give him mine, then?" Narinder wiped hers with a polishing cloth and held it out to Paula.

"No, it's ..."

"Yeah, go on. Do a swap. Be my present to your grandad."

"Eh?"

"*Please.*" And Narinder meant it; she wasn't just being kind.

"You sure? He'd love it, comin' from you."

"No, tell him you done it. He'll feel proud, you sort of following in his footsteps. While he's ill, eh ...?" It seemed a good idea to Narinder, who'd been giving a lot of thought to the need to please grandparents, all of a sudden.

"I dunno." Paula fingered the spoon, looked around for Mr Woodruff in case he saw what was going on. "All right," she said. "Ta, Nind. I'll do something for you one day."

"Yeah, I might hold you to that, girl."

"You do."

A repaid favour which really didn't seem all that likely, just then, as the bell went and the two girls packed up to go home to their separate problems.

"Come on, Dad, try and perk up. Dolly's coming over in a bit. Be nice to see her, eh?"

Sam was lying back in bed, his head sinking back into the pillow deeper by the day.

"I feel wrung out ... like ... an old dish-cloth," he told his daughter-in-law as she plumped the pillows under his head, nodding him up and down like a pathetic puppet.

"I know. I'll have a word with Dolly. Perhaps we'll get the doctor in again. But he said to give it a day or two on those tablets."

Sam sighed, turned his head to one side, staring, like someone ready to give up. "I don't feel very well," he said, feebly.

But Ellie didn't reply; wasn't listening; she'd just heard the clatter of a taxi's diesel and she was over at the curtains, looking out. "Oh, I don't believe it! They're here already." She looked at the old-fashioned alarm clock on Sam's bedside table. "Tttt! Bang on the minute, as per usual," she complained. "You could set your blessed video by them." And giving a quick dust to his musical box she shot out of the room without another glance towards him.

It was all smiles down at the front door; the sort that show the teeth. "Hello, Deany, Paula . . . Dolly, love. You got away on time, then, Mick?"

But Dolly cut through the tangle of greetings. "How's he been today, Ellie? I'm so blessed worried. . ."

Ellie's face took on the pained look of someone who doesn't feel the pain. "Poor old Dad. See what you think, but he can't seem ever to lose that headache, and sometimes it's so. . ." she looked at the children and dropped her voice . . . "*acute.*"

"What's the doctor say?"

Ellie pursed her lips, motioned for Dolly and Mick to come into the kitchen. "Deany, Uncle's got some new videos in the den." She turned to Paula, clearly not sure whether she was to be an adult or a child.

But Paula knew what she was all right. "Can I go straight up?" she asked.

"Help yourself, love. He's all neat and tidy."

The others went into the kitchen while Paula, with Narinder's spoon warm in her hand, ran up the stairs to her grandad's room. She knew what she was. Too right! More grown-up than any of them downstairs, because she was grown-up in a real sense, the life-and-death sense of the world of rackets. There weren't many people right now, not politicians, not police, definitely not teachers, who were sitting on the sort of secret she was.

She peeped into Sam's bedroom. "'Lo Grandad!" She ran over and kissed him, with love, and with care. "How you doin'?"

She saw him trying to put on a smile. "Oh, not so dusty, love . . ."

"Brought you something. What I made." She gave him Narinder's spoon, watched his face, desperately wanted him to be proud of her.

The old man tried to focus his eyes on it, up close. "'Ere, you done that well," he said. "What is it?" But the laugh which went with his joke seemed to hurt him too much and he ended up wincing in pain.

"No, tell you the truth, I never made it. Nindy did. She wanted you to have it." Paula gabbled on, just for something to do while he went through the spasm.

But Sam had let the spoon drop and was trying to pull himself up. It was as if the latest blinding pain had given him something urgent to do: but the effort pushed his head back in defeat.

"Gawd, girl, I dunno where to put myself."

Paula sat on the edge of the bed and stroked his hot forehead. He'd gone downhill so fast! In under a week he'd become a different person.

He made another attempt to sit up, was staring at his musical box across the room, weakly flapping a hand at it.

"Yeah, a nice tune on your musical box, eh?" Paula got up. "It did use to help old Nan . . ." But with her back to him as she went over to it she didn't see the sudden anguished look on his face, the struggle he was having to tell her something.

"Come here," his hand rose, and fell under its own weight. And as Paula turned then she knew that it wasn't any tune he wanted.

"The mess . . ."

"The mess? The *message*!" Paula was back on the bed and cuddling him close to her, cradling his head and bending her ear to his lips. But they were only quivering now, hardly moving. "What? Eh? What, Grandad?"

But there was no reply. And in that moment Paula suddenly grew up in another way, in a way that can happen without the benefit of a warning, and always irrespective of age. She found herself cradling a man's head as he died. With a sudden, short snoring sound, body deep, Sam stared at her, and with his mouth stretched open as if he were desperate for one last gasp of living air, his head fell back and an armistice settled his pain.

"Grandad! Grandad! You all right?" But Paula knew only too well that he wasn't: she knew what had happened: and with a mix of fear at her grandad being dead in her arms and yet not wanting to let him go, she eased her hand out from under his head and ran to scream for her mother from the top of the stairs.

six

Elkin didn't bat an eye when Brian Butler went to the bingo to tell him that the old man had died out at Ilford. If he'd thought he was due some sort of a pat on the back he was in for a shock. Because all that his bounce showed was that he hadn't understood the problem. "Get the glasses, find out where they are," he'd been told, "use your family ties to trip him up." But all Brian really knew was how to steal a car and how to lean on people. He hadn't understood why Elkin hadn't just had Sam put out of the way: he hadn't grasped the fact that Sam had got a hidden ace he could play even after he was dead. So the cocky smile and the slight waggle of the head as he told Elkin the news were quickly replaced by a look of surprise and a jump to attention when Leila started shouting at him.

"Are you as stupid as you look?" she demanded. "This is what we never wanted, him dead! Now we've got to sweat on nothing happening . . ."

But Elkin, although he wasn't delighted at Brian's news, didn't seem quite so worried. "No. They know it weren't us. Doctor'll prove that. It was natural. We're O.K., I reckon. But now we gotta be clever, that's how I see it."

Brian nodded. The way Elkin saw things was the way you did, too.

" 'Cos he's still protecting the girl and all the rest of the family. He's still left a message somewhere saying where them glasses are . . ."

"In his will at the bank?" Brian interrupted, trying to make up for being an idiot.

"Not been touched since the robbery." Elkin swore. "I said we gotta be clever, not bleedin' *obvious*. No, he's left word in some funny place, in some funny way." He took his new glasses off, huffed on them, polished them with a silk handkerchief while he thought. "Now, you're round all the family, son. And very upset times, funerals are. So if you want being kept on, you're gonna keep your eyes and ears open and you're gonna find out where he's left that word, right? Someone knows, you can bet your life on that . . ."

Brian nodded, eagerly. "Yeah, yeah, O.K., Mr Elkin."

"Right. Then you toddle off an' buy a nice black tie and armband. Get to your funeral and see what else comes pouring out besides tears!"

"Will do, Mr Elkin. No sweat, I won't let you down."

"No? You'd better not, son, I tell you . . ."

And Brian went; definitely a lot more hot and bothered than when he'd jauntily driven in with the sad news.

Paula had never been to a funeral before. She'd been too young to go to her nan's, the way Dean was too young for their grandad's. She hadn't even known how to get ready for it in her mind. What did they do at a funeral? What did you see? Would she be frightened? And how would her mum and uncle take it? Would she be able to stand all the crying? Could she cope with her own sadness? But when the dreadful day came and she waited in her black at Uncle Frank's, given the job of writing down the names on the floral tributes as they were spread out on the front lawns, what took her completely by surprise was the way she was one of the centres of attention. At previous family things like this the children were usually left to keep quiet and behave themselves: but today at her grandad's funeral everyone came over to give her a kiss and a special squeeze, just as much as they did to her mother. And apart from her loutish cousin Brian keeping staring at her with his wet mouth open, she felt wanted and warmed and comforted. It all made her grandad's final send-off that much easier to take.

Frank had found a vicar who sounded as if he cared: and he did well, got everyone's name right, didn't leave out a single name which should have had a mention. And in words which choked Paula, he paid tribute to this 'fine father and husband, this loving grandad, this much-loved man'. She'd been in some sort of control till then, with Mick taking care of her: numbed by her first sight of the coffin in the hearse, by how small a box they could get such a big man in; but at the sound of the word 'grandad' she broke up: and her shoulders hardly stopped heaving, her red face throbbing, until the grim business with the lowering of the coffin and the clattering of the earth on its lid had been done, and they had helped one another in slow cuddles back to the cars.

The line of black ribboned cabs set eyes turning all along the Romford Road, and back at the house everything seemed to have moved into a sort of a dream, like being in a film, till a rap on the sideboard and a sudden shout lifted Paula's eyes from her Auntie Ellie's deep-pile carpet, and she returned to the reality of it all, the noise, the drinks, the laughing even, which had surfaced now that her grandad was somewhere else. And here was Uncle Frank, with a long, white envelope in one hand, a cut-glass scotch in the other, and an important look in his eye.

"Now, if I can have a bit of order, please . . ."

"Best of order, everyone!"

Frank looked round, waited for everyone's attention.

"I think the vicar, Mr Spinks, said everything we wanted said, back at the chapel," he told them all. "My sad duty now concerns our dad's will." He shivered it in his hand, to let everyone see how legal it looked. "Now, what he's done – I won't read it out – is to leave everything to us two, that's Dolly and me, to dispose of as we see fit . . ." He looked round the room as if daring anyone to contest the fairness of that. "All here in black and white, duly witnessed." He turned to pay special attention to a settee of Sam's brothers and sisters.

"Naturally, we'll make sure everyone gets a nice little keepsake when we've sorted through. But there is one little, er, extra clause. About Mum's musical box." And the settee perked up, just for a second. *"Which he's left to Paula."*

Paula caught her breath, taken completely by surprise. She certainly hadn't expected to hear her name called out. She looked up and frowned, tried to recall what had just been said. Had she heard it right? But Uncle Frank had already turned to the sideboard, opened a door and carefully taken out the musical box which he carried to her across the room. "He wanted you to have it, my love."

His voice had caught and there were fresh tears in his eyes as he handed the heavy instrument down to her.

"Me? Did he say that?" She looked over to Dolly for confirmation. Eyes closing, mouth pursed, her mother nodded back.

"It's in a codicil to the will. And it couldn't go to a nicer kid." Uncle Frank kissed her on the forehead, hugged her round the shoulders as she sat cradling the box, and now she began to cry again. "I'm very happy for you," he tried to say. Then, composing himself, he stood up and concluded for the rest of the room: "So! The reading of the will."

The conversation picked up then, and louder than before. Mick and Frank got the drinks going again, Dolly and Ellie ran in and out of the room carrying hot sausage rolls which nobody was allowed to refuse: while Paula sat and stroked the pattern on the inlaid lid of her special gift from her grandad. To her it was somehow as if, having left him behind in that deep grave, he'd forgiven her for coming back to the house without him. "Oh, Grandad," she rocked and stroked. "Oh, Grandad."

But a sudden sense told her that someone was there, waiting at her side to have a word. She looked up. It was her cousin Brian, much the worse for wear.

"Nice, i'n it?" he said in a slurred voice, his mouth going like a frog's. And his nail-bitten fingers flipped up the lid, his dry eyes stared inside. "Ain't you the chosen little cousin?" he sneered. "Paula, love! Now I jus' wonder why . . . ?"

It was never a consolation – Paula could never be consoled about her grandad's death – but as well as inheriting the musical box she did get her bedroom back. They gave it a week or so, then Mick stripped it out and made it hers again: new paper, a new rug, and a little unit he made with lights, like in an actress's dressing room. Not, he told her, that he wanted to get rid of her grandad's memory, but there was no way they had to keep his room like a shrine to remember him; and he did want Paula to feel that it was hers. As for the speed he did it with – well, once the room was vacant it was amazing how many rows Dean had with her over the room they shared. Funny, Paula thought, how quickly problems crop up once there's a way to sort them out. And now, while the paint and the paper still smelt fresh, it was a place of her own, where Paula could have Nindy without watching every word: and where she could cry if she wanted, without Dean telling her she was only putting it on. And she cried a lot, sitting on the patterned duvet, playing her musical box.

"It's no good, Nind," she said one afternoon when they'd been let out early and Nindy wouldn't be missed. "My dad's tried, but I still think of Grandad in here."

Narinder put an arm round her: gave her friend a hug. "Poor old Paula. Wish I could make you feel better."

Paula suddenly snapped herself out of it. Grief came and went like that, could be handled in small amounts. "Look at me – you got enough on your own plate. But Nind, what am I gonna do if you go an' all?"

Narinder didn't want to go into that, though. She wasn't sure she could handle it. "He's giving in!" It was anger, not self-pity. "The more people give in to them crooks the worse they get."

"'S what I said . . . "

"It's true, I'm not just saying it." Narinder's years as an Asian Londoner had taught her that you couldn't afford to pretend not to hear what was said nor to see what went on: if her generation was ever to have a chance it had to brave things out, stand up to them whatever it cost.

"I'm not just saying it, Nind," Paula impressed. "I *know* about some of them ..."

Which made Narinder sit up and listen. So were there more than just the Asians who were getting the treatment? "How d'you mean?" But even as she stared, asked with her eyes, Paula suddenly backed off; moved away physically to get at the musical box handle, and smiled.

"Oh – you know," she said. "Here, you heard this one? It's got a real catchy tune ..." And she played one of the Gilbert and Sullivan marches on the spiky prongs. "Nice, i'n it?" she asked.

But Narinder was more interested in her friend's red face, and the bit of quick back-tracking she'd just done.

While the girls were playing the musical box in Paula's bedroom, Brian was making a thorough search of that other room of Sam's, the one he'd died in. Ellie and Frank had gone through it in the normal sorting-out way, clearing out the old man's clothes; and Ellie had given it one of her spring cleans, to get the death out of the corners, as she said. But no-one had done to that room what they'd done at Paula's house, turned it over for anything Elkin might want, and now Brian was making sure. With his mother out at the hairdresser's and his father busy at the showroom, he'd booked himself out to go and look at a couple of motors on offer but driven himself home instead. Now, alone in the house, he could be as thorough as he liked.

But as it turned out he didn't have to be. He didn't have to have the carpet up, crawling on hands and knees looking for chipped floorboard cracks: he didn't even have to look for sewing marks on the mattress cover: because what he was looking for was in a much more straightforward place than that, deep down behind the radiator, wrapped in two dusters. The moment he saw it he shouted, "Gotcha!" and within minutes he was racing through the rush-hour streets to find Elkin.

"I think I'm on to it, Mr Elkin. The clue, you know..." Brian slid his suitcase onto the pub table and almost had Elkin's tonic water over.

"Don't tell the world," the big man said, flatly.

Brian didn't risk saying anything more. He opened the brief-case and laid what he had found on the table. Slowly he unwrapped the dusters for Elkin to stare at the thirty centimetre steel cylinder with the lines of fine prickles standing up off its surface.

"What the hell is it?" The man sipped his drink slowly. "It looks bloody lethal."

"He made it. He was good at this sort of thing. It's a thingy, a barrel, a cylinder, like – for a musical box..."

"Yeah? So what's that got to do with what I want?"

Brian leaned over, beside himself. "The old man had a musical box, took it everywhere with him. But I swear this ain't the cylinder in it. That one's brass. Like I said, he's made this himself..."

"So, he was a composer..." Elkin did his Jewish comedian voice.

"Mr Elkin, what I reckon is, putting two and two together, he's made this new one with some special tune on it; see, something someone's gonna know. And that'll give the clue to where he's hidden your ... *you know what* ..." He looked across at the powerful man, like a dog looking up for a pat.

"A musical clue, is that what you're trying to say? Sounds like some telly game."

"I know. But see, he could do this sort of thing."

"And what tune is it, then? What's the word, what's the

message?" Elkin turned to a crossword in the *Evening Standard*, looked as though the black and white squares held a lot more interest for him than Brian's going-on.

"I dunno. I haven't played it yet."

"Oh, you haven't?" Elkin stared at the red-face boy. "Just rushed round here at half-cock instead?" He clicked his fingers for another drink, which came before he'd written in the next word.

Brian's voice went nervous-high, the way scared apologies do. "Well, I haven't got the musical box it fits. Not no more. My cousin's got it. Paula Prescott. The old boy left it to her in his will."

Elkin stirred the drink with his biro, made the tonic fizz on the ice. "Well, you'd better get it back off her, then, son. Hadn't you? Don't see much use of one without the other. Like having a video without a machine, seems to me. Pretty bloody *useless*."

And with *useless* ringing loud round the bar, Brian was left to edge away, all polite smiles, and take out his temper on the door of his car.

Narinder was with Paula in the school playground when Brian drove up the next day. The girls were near the railings, talking about a new album, finding things to say that wouldn't worsen their depressions when out of the side of her eye Narinder saw a man get out of a car, come over the pavement towards the railings, lean an arm through and slowly beckon her towards him. It was scary, and in that moment, as his face came into focus, it suddenly hit her who he was. The man in the shop! The man with the ink! Her heart missed a beat and her stomach seemed to drop away inside her. *The protection bloke!* He'd come to get her. Her father hadn't paid, and now what he'd been scared of was coming true. The man had come to pay them a lesson!

So what should she do? She wanted to scream, but she tried

to focus on thinking, just to stop herself walking towards him like a hypnotised rabbit. *Should* she go to him, or turn and run – zig-zag through the playground to try to lose herself? In a panic, she looked about. Were there any more of them around, already inside the gate? She stared at Paula, opened her mouth, wanted to say something but suddenly couldn't find the words.

And then the man called, waving his arm more wildly. "Paula! *Paula*! Deaf-ears, you! Over 'ere! I want you a minute!"

Paula? Was this some kind of a mixed-up nightmare? Narinder watched her friend turn round and see the man herself; heard her say in a very normal voice, no worse than finding some door shut, "Oh, hello, what's up with him? Won't be a minute, Nind," and run over to the railings, get close enough to the crook for him to grab her if he'd wanted and *talk* to him. Narinder couldn't believe it. Couldn't believe what she was seeing. Paula didn't look frightened, even seemed to know him: then off he went, with a crooked sort of smile; and Paula came back pulling a nasty-taste face of her own: but definitely nothing serious: definitely a long way from a life and death matter . . .

"Paula, that bloke – what's he want with you?" Hard as she tried Narinder couldn't keep the tremble out of her voice.

"Only passing. Great galoot. Wanted a word with my dad over something. Wanted to know if he was home today, or if his cab was in dock."

Narinder felt the drying as her mouth dropped open. "You know him, then? That bloke?" She watched with Paula as the car revved away.

"Yeah, 'course I do – he's my cousin, isn't he? Brian. The toe-rag. The horrible Brian!"

It was all true. Your legs did go weak at moments like this. "Your *cousin*?" Narinder somehow got out.

"Yeah. Why? What's up? What you looking at me like that for? Nindy!"

But Narinder Kaur Sidhu couldn't answer: instead, she took a grip of the top of a five-a-side goal and used it to steady herself while she stared at her old friend, at Paula Prescott, the one she'd come up through the primary school with, the friend she'd been so close to it was almost like being married: and in that long moment of incredulous staring she realised the awful truth about her. All this time there'd been something she hadn't known: all this time the girl had been covering up that she was from a family of villains, covering up being from a family on the other side – had fooled her nicely, probably fed stuff back to the people who were behind her own father being so scared. And she'd done it all right – up till now, when that villain had stupidly shown himself for some reason. Oh, God! It was like a kick in the heart: the most painful blow she'd ever felt.

She found some words. No breath, but some words, very weak, but with all the ferocity seven years of being betrayed can give.

"You! Prescott! You ... rotten ... little ... traitor!" And stopping herself from starting a fight by only the finest thread of control, she ran off into the school, eyes blind with tears, colliding with everyone in her path.

seven

How Narinder ever got to the library she didn't know. Tempers were usually on such short fuses at Goldings that someone would be set off by being bumped into. And in the disbelieving rage she was in she couldn't even see where she was going properly. She was shattered by what had happened; she couldn't come to grips with it. Paula Prescott, a good old heart-of-gold East End mate had suddenly turned out to be part of a family all tied up with Elkin and his rackets – and she'd never guessed, not in all those years. She must've been stupid, Narinder thought, all that time since the Infants – going to Prescott's house, telling her all her own secrets and never knowing this one back. And what she just couldn't come to grips with, in the past few weeks, was that while she'd been letting on to the girl about how up against it her family was, how she was being sent to her grandparents in India as soon as the money could be raised, that little rat had been on the other side all the time! It was shattering: like being in a bomb blast and thrown off your feet to go skittling across the playground, all numbed by shock.

All she knew now was that she had to find somewhere quiet, had to put her head in her hands, and cry, and just *think*. But the classrooms were locked and the lavatories stank; so the only place was the library.

She pushed herself in there, still not seeing straight, walked smack into a paperback carousel. But the office was empty, and the only person there to stare was a prefect writing an essay or some love letter in a corner.

Narinder went up to the other end, pulled out any old book

and slumped herself down at a table. The high bookshelves hid her from the rest of the room, the prefect didn't know her, and if she didn't make too much noise about it she could stay there and just let it all come out. But now that they could, the tears wouldn't come. The trembling did, the anger, the thumps on the table with her fists – but her eyes had dried, and they stayed dry. It was as if this feeling she had, this huge emotion, was just too enormous to be shown by any minor reaction of the body. *Shock* was the word for it: a state of shock: she'd heard it said often enough and now she knew what it meant. And it *was* enormous, what had happened. The awful, sudden knowing that in all the world you're absolutely on your own is too big to take in just like that. Not having anyone to turn to who is on your side is about the loneliest you can ever be: let alone not even having anyone you can *imagine* telling your troubles to.

Narinder's eyes stared at the shelves: they saw the irrelevant titles – *Discovering London, Old Father Thames*: she sighed in a deep sort of hopelessness at being surrounded by books which were no longer anything to do with her. So what did they matter now? she asked herself in her misery. It had never been a bowl of roses, being an Asian in this part of the world, it had always been more a bed of nettles; being the target for so much ignorant hatred. But it had been what she'd grown up to, and London had been her place. And she'd always had a mum and a dad who loved her – they'd done things together, gone to the gurdwara, had laughs and cries together – which was a lot more to have than tons of kids she knew. Now all that was coming to an end – they'd got so scared over what might happen they wouldn't listen to her begging to let her stay: so from living a London life with people she loved she was being sent somewhere strange and foreign, where she might know the religion and some of the words but she definitely didn't know the ways. Which was how those books on London had mattered up to today. They'd summed up what she'd had, and they'd summed up what she could lose.

But now – *but now*! Narinder lifted her eyes to the ceiling as if she were looking to God for some sort of help. But now this terrible, deep, sinking feeling told her that she might as well go, lose it all: because there was nothing to stay here for, not any more, not when her one life-long friend had betrayed her. Not when she wouldn't even want to be waved goodbye by anyone.

She heard the sounds of the school: the screams and shouts and laughs of kids in the playground, the scrape of violins from somewhere, and a smoker's cough. She smelt the smell of the place – the paper and print that was in the library, that special smell that summed up her life because it was also in her hair and her clothes from home: the smell of words. All this about her – and she didn't have a soul in the world to talk to.

"Nind!"

Narinder swung round, saw who was there, who she knew would be there sooner or later, putting on a show of being all innocent. She stuck her head back in the book she wasn't reading.

"Nindy! What the 'ell was all that?"

The response was a shift away, head deeper into the book.

"You gotta tell me! You can't suddenly just turn..."

"Hey, you!" Paula was interrupted, but not by Narinder – by the prefect who had stood up to where he could see them. "Go an' talk in the yard." He gave them a look and sat down again.

Paula lowered her voice, slid in opposite. "Nindy!"

Narinder just raised her eyes, let the accusation too big for words stare out at the white-faced girl.

"Wassup, Nind?"

"Don't you come all innocent. You want me to spell it out for you?"

"You want a detention?" The boy was getting angry now.

But Paula was getting angry too – or pretending to. Raising her voice, anyhow. "Someone'd better start spellin' it out, girl, or I'll start thinking I'm going *mad*!" She tried to put her hand on Narinder's. "You're my best mate, Nindy."

"*Was* your best mate!" Narinder's hand flew away at the touch, like flesh touched by fire. "They all said I was stupid to go on trustin' a white girl." She screwed up her eyes. "Why don't you go back to your rotten crook out there, to your dear cousin and be his best mate! 'Ave a laugh with him. Ask him when he's coming to put the wind up my dad again. I know your rotten family now!" Slamming the book shut she thought of throwing it at Paula; but instead she slapped it down hard and loud on the table and stood up. "Get out the way, Prescott!"

The other girl looked as if she was staring at a death: mouth open, eyes without a blink left in them: looking at Narinder as if she'd gone completely mad. But as Narinder scraped chairs and pushed at the table to get out of Paula's sight the prefect suddenly stood in her way. "I've warned you! What's your name?" he demanded.

And Narinder lost it – that tensile wire of control finally snapped. "She'll tell you!" she screamed in his face. "*My* name, she will!" She started sobbing, spat words at him and swung round to point an angry, shaking finger at Paula. "But don't ask hers for crissake or she'll send the mafia round!" And with a strength she didn't have, she pushed the prefect out of her way and ran for the library door.

Dolly Prescott was out of mourning now. As she sat at her desk at Frank Butler Motors her nails shone red against the black of the typewriter keyboard, her hair and her dress looking as if she might as easily have got up and given a song. She had a poise which said she was used to seeing her reflection in windscreens, breathing in the smell of these polished luxury models: that she knew her shoes had to outshine tyres like jet. And it said that she enjoyed working at the top end of the market; liked the idea that people never *needed* to have a Frank

Butler Motor, didn't come in as if they were replacing a Hoover or arranging a funeral, but more in an act of love. Behind her, in his partitioned office, her brother Frank was arranging finance for a man who'd fallen in love with a Rover. Every so often he looked up, as if he were checking that no other potential customer was slipping away: because Brian wasn't there – he was up to something, hadn't been seen since first thing – and Frank was in a mood. On top of which the customer in with him right now was bent on having a car they could sell a hundred times over, when they'd thought he'd taken a shine to a sticking Daimler.

Dolly ripped a contract out of her machine, screwed it up and started again. As she dusted her hands of the carbon, she looked up. Brian had come in carrying something big and heavy in a carrier bag. "All right, Dolly?" he asked.

"I am," Dolly told him. "But you'd better watch out. Your dad's been looking for you." She turned her attention back to the new contract form as Brian went round behind her towards the workshop door.

"Picked up a Bentley dynamo," he said. "Take a bit of finding, these do. . ." He paused and looked all about him, his eyes starting and finishing with Dolly – then in one swift and silent movement he dropped her door key into the pocket of her hanging sheepskin. "Can't be everywhere at once!" he told her.

The bus home from Goldings School was its usual clattering, swaying place. They came on like the Normandy landings and took seats, set up territories with all the manoeuvring of marines. As a rule, Paula and Narinder would have been with them, anxious to get a double seat. But today had become different already, and it was going to be different here. After an afternoon in school where they'd been forced to be close, all sighs and turned backs, Narinder was free to choose now – and getting up the stairs ahead of Paula she found an outside seat and pointedly put her bag on the window one.

"Charming!" Paula wrinkled her nose and found a seat of her own. But Tommy and Scott, never far behind, read something else into the new arrangements.

"Hey, Scotty! They saved our places. One each!" And before Narinder could do anything about it, Tommy had shoved her over and thumped himself down next to her.

Scott, never so sure, sat carefully next to Paula and started to pretend a deep interest out of the opposite window.

"Knew you'd come round in the end," Tommy started telling Narinder. "Couldn't resist, eh? Or 'ave you two had a bust-up?"

Narinder looked round at him, the brash boy who thought he only had to wiggle his finger: and at first she thought she wouldn't even bother to answer: the great lug, who did he think he was, doing her a favour? But as she looked at him she saw that Paula was in her line of vision, too. Prescott the traitor being ignored by Scott; her so-called best friend, who right now was keen as mustard to find out what was going on over here … All right! she suddenly thought. Why not? Let the little worm see how quick I can dry my eyes! And making sure the girl could see, she turned to Tommy and gave him a new smile she'd just found from somewhere.

And when you actually looked at him he wasn't a bad looking boy! she thought. A bit less mouth and he'd be all right. Besides – she started to get excited by the idea – so what? Her going to India any time, being let down like that, what did it matter who she liked or what she did? Let the Asians stare. Did she have to worry what people thought any more? And, to be honest, it was quite nice, Tommy sitting close, better than Prescott; and even the way he'd gone a bit red, well, that was nice, too. No, she thought, why shouldn't she enjoy it? Because when had she last enjoyed anything, really?

"Here, Nind, look what I've been saving up for you." Out of his top pocket Tommy suddenly slid two tickets, printed up the way her father did, all swirls and gilt. "Disco, down the Wakefield Centre." He held them in his fingers, twirled them at her like a conjurer with playing cards. She took the tickets and looked. It was a Church Army Youth Club disco to be held at their headquarters on the Barking Road, all straight and above board, an International Night. Narinder sighed and pulled a face. Last year her father might have taken some persuading, she'd have had to go with Paula, but she would have gone in the end: now, though, it was very different.

"When is this?"

Tommy pointed out the date. "Tonight. Short notice." He leaned in closer till she could smell the spearmint on his breath. "Still – why not? Show ol' Prescott she ain't the only fish on the slab."

Narinder looked over at her former girlfriend, turned back to look the boy in the eye. Was that why he was asking her? Because it was quite something for round here, she thought – a Sikh girl being asked out by a white boy.

"Come on! I ain't National Front. Pretty girl's a pretty girl, i'nt she? See you outside the *Denmark* at seven. Eh?" Then he put an arm round her and squeezed: a physical thing, and new, and exciting – just the warm feel of another person she needed in the middle of all her isolation.

"Yeah! All right, I'll try." She pushed his arm away before someone started making anything of it. "Got nothing to lose, have I?"

"Great!" Tommy said, getting all bouncy. "You try hard, eh?"

To which Narinder, making sure that Paula could see, sparkled her eyes and gave him another of those special new smiles she'd just found.

Paula trailed home off the bus, taking the right turnings automatically, not knowing how she got there. She couldn't think straight. Her throat hurt, her Adam's apple was swollen with injustice and not crying, her stomach was numb, and a tight feeling choked her chest at the grief, the new mourning at the loss of this other person she'd used to think she loved.

But how could Nindy have ever dared to call herself a friend? Who the hell did she think she was, shouting at her, accusing her of being a crook? What the devil had she been on about at school? It was like she'd suddenly got into some religious trance and lost her mind.

And then on the bus! Squeezing up close to Tommy, showing off like some sixth-form girl with a teacher. It just wasn't *true*, it was like she'd suddenly changed into someone else.

Anyhow, Paula decided, no-one did that sort of thing to her! Not twice! She'd give as good as she got tomorrow – *and* get some change!

With a bang and a slam she let herself into the house. Her mother wasn't in yet, but Dean was, taking up the lounge as usual. Getting herself a glass of Coke, she gave him an accidental kick where his leg was in her way, and while he was still shouting and hollering at her, she cleared off to her own room, just to be where no-one could see her. She threw herself down on the bed, turned over, stared at the ceiling, got up, opened some drawers, closed them, sat, stood, wandered, brushed her hair, tried on some ear-rings, fingered her 'Paula' necklace – and with a big, sad sigh, went to wind-up her musical box.

Went to – but didn't, because when she focused on the dresser top, actually concentrated on it, there was the place, four little circles where the rubber feet went, but the musical box itself had gone – been moved somewhere. Paula swore. That Dean! He'd been in here again, playing some sort of stupid game. Probably captured it from some enemy, his ammunition or gold, hidden it away where they couldn't find it, the idiot ... Well, she'd show him! How dare he come into her room! Wound up now with frustration and anger, she charged down the stairs to have it out with him. And it took a lot of shouting and a raining of blows in both directions for the truth to come out. He hadn't touched the thing, wouldn't go near it if anyone paid him a million pounds. And while the tears and the insults were still flowing, their mother slammed in and roasted them both.

"As if life isn't hard enough! Out to work all day and I come in to this! Just you wait till your father gets in!"

But by the time Mick was expected, they were all waiting for him for a different reason. They were hoping he'd solve the mystery of the missing musical box. "He did say he'd have it valued one day," Paula had said – and now she was praying that this had been the day: because they'd searched every-where – and with nothing else gone from the house, it was the only possible explanation.

But all Mick carried in with him when he came was his takings pouch – which he threw, light as pitta onto the settee. "I won't get a rupture carrying that!" he snorted. "I'm going into the shoe repair business. Everyone's blinkin' walking these days!"

Dolly stared at him, ventured the words like lifting a sharp tin lid. "Mick, I know we're pushed, love ... but you haven't gone and. . .? Not with Paula's. . .?"

"Do what?"

Puffy-eyed, thick in the throat, her head beginning to ache with all the emotions of the loss and the rows, Paula put it to him straight. "Dad – did you take my musical box this morning?"

"Eh? I got a cab radio," Mick joked. "Imagine me – " But he didn't get far, and no-one did for a while. Because when the story came out and Mick had had his shout and checked the doors and the windows for signs of intrusion, the house was gone over as thoroughly as Elkin's gang had gone over it – and of the musical box there was not a sign.

Everything came back to Paula's bedroom.'

"It was definitely on there," she told Mick and Dolly.

Dolly nodded. "I saw it when I made the bed this morning. Had a little tear ..."

"And none of the windows 'as been forced." Mick double-checked Paula's. "So it's definitely got to be a key job."

"Well, who else has got a key, then, apart from us?" And suddenly, Dolly froze. "No! Oh, no!" She turned to stare in horror at her husband. "Mick! My key. Today. I thought I must've been going potty. At work, I definitely left it in my handbag. But coming home, it was in my pocket. Thought it was funny, but then I walked into this, and – "

Mick was shaking his head. "I don't see that, Doll. What would Frank want, monkeying about with your key? He'd ask you, wouldn't he, if he wanted something round here?"

Paula thought about her Uncle Frank; thought about his kind smile, his nice words and his hug when he'd given her the musical box. He *had* wanted her to have it, been so kind handing it over without any fuss. He wouldn't have wanted it back. But suddenly, Paula frowned. There was someone who hadn't been so pleased, wasn't there? What about that jealous face her cousin had pulled? Rotten Brian?

"Hang on a minute!" It just burst out, never mind sounding like rubbish. "What about Brian? If Uncle Frank could've got Mum's key then Brian could've, couldn't he?" And all at once the rest came back. "*And he was round my school dinner-time!* First time ever. Wanted to know was Dad in!"

"Eh? Really?" Mick's face had taken on that schoolboy boxing champion look, that special set of the jaw for when people looked like not wanting to pay a fare. "Well, would you ...?! I'll have him! I will, the little toe-rag! I'll soon sort him, and Frank, 'cos I ain't bloomin' having this!"

Mick punched his palm, Dolly stared. But it was Paula who it got to most: since into her head had just come the memory of some of the things Narinder had said about Brian: and for one horrible, clear moment they suddenly seemed to start to fit...

Brian's ears were certainly burning at the time: but not so much at being talked about by the Prescotts as at the roasting Elkin was giving him down the phone. With careful, car-thief fingers he had unscrewed the hundred-year-old brass cylinder from its bed in the musical box, and in its place, fitting perfectly, he had fixed the cylinder he had found. The spiky notes on this new one didn't cover the full range that the old one did, they were grouped more in the middle, but the cylinder fitted perfectly, and now he'd phoned to let Elkin know. But all he got was a slagging off. Why hadn't he tried it out? Why didn't he know what the message was? What was the use of reporting that he'd *half* done something?

"Make a tape of it!" Elkin shouted down the phone. "And lose that musical box 'fore someone else gets bright ideas! Christ 'ave I got to do all your thinking for you?" At the end of which Brian heard only a click – but the slam of the phone could almost be felt through the ground.

"Bloody Grandad!" he shouted. "Why d'you have to get all mixed up in this?"

Narinder had had her moments of anger as well, her outbursts at the traitorous and unfair world. But now her mood was emptier, depressed, and just at that moment she felt sick, too, at the sight of her clothes, her saris, salvar kameez and dupattas laundered for packing, blowing on the line in their narrow back garden. She crunched, heel-toe, heel-toe along the cinder path, head down, seeing nothing. She heard her mother come out of the house, wobbling the empty plastic basket for the washing, and yet she didn't hear her. There wasn't a sight or a sound in the whole world that could give her a lift.

"Let down the line, Narinder, it's getting damp."

Narinder heard the Punjabi words and mechanically, with heavy hands, she unwound the thin rope from the cleats.

"How about stringing me up with the next lot?" she asked, in English.

Kamal bustled in a matter-of-fact way, clearly wasn't going to take such depressing talk seriously. "No, the rope would break and all the clean clothes get muddy."

"It's not funny."

A clothes-peg sprung sideways out of Kamal's fingers, hit the fence with a click. "So when was the last time you saw me laughing?"

Narinder looked at the tired eyes, the transparent skin, the mouth that only spoke and ate these days. What a long way from the beautiful bride of the picture album. And what a lifetime from looking at it that day with Prescott . . .

"Everything's gone rotten."

"For all of us, Nindy, not only for you."

"But — " Narinder waved at the clothes on the line, the symbol of what she was going to have to become.

"We are Sikh, Narinder, and Sikhs are proud people. If we cannot stay, then we go, proudly. . ."

"Oh, come on!" Narinder hated hearing her mother talk like this: because she was doing no more than echoing her father, talking of pride but acting out defeat. It was all words, excuses, wrapped up in sugar paper. "I'm proud, too, you know — and Sikh. I do all you do, I read the granth, I go down the gurdwara — but the difference is, I'm English Sikh, see?" She hurt herself, poking her own chest so hard with her finger. "I'm a new sort. You're Punjab Sikh, and I'm London Sikh." She raised her voice, pleaded. "It's different. . ."

But Kamal stayed very calm, heard it out before she quietly dropped in a word, like a teacher. "But what when London isn't wanting you?"

"Sewer rats of London never wanted us. This is a gang, it's for the money. . ."

"No, Nindy, it's a white gang — it's more than money underneath. . ."

This was the sort of talk that made Narinder mad.

"Nothing gets better if you run! I got white friends! My best friend's..." And there she suddenly faltered, because in the heat of the dispute she'd forgotten for the moment where she stood with Paula Prescott. She slammed her mouth shut: but riding on the tail of that depressing thought there had come another, something more cheerful. "There's *some* in London want me," she said. She looked at her watch. What time had Tommy said?

"And many others who are not wanting you. It's the story of the world, Narinder. You learn in the end that your own people, your own family, will always be there, on your side. But even your closest friend, my father used to say, is always a river away."

Narinder shut her mouth again and listened.

"On the other side of the water, Nindy."

Narinder nodded. But only briefly. Because with talk of rivers came the thought of the Punjab, the region of five rivers: and it had suddenly struck her that time was running very short for her. Quickly, she walked away from the clothes line, the saris, the salvar kameez, the dupattas, and headed indoors for something else that was hanging in her wardrobe: something that would be just right for one of her final flings in London ...

Brian Butler's bedroom was a temple to white violence. As well as the weight-lifting bench and the bull-worker for packing his own pale flesh with muscle, the room boasted great posters of white boxers and Hollywood gangsters. The lampshade was a Union Jack and the one football scarf said West Ham. But the music being played in it that night sounded vaguely Indian, and it was coming from the newly-fitted cylinder in the musical box – producing a rhythm and a tonal quality which fitted more the sitar and the raga than the military march or music hall tune of tradition. Which left

Brian, hearing it for the fourth time, on the edge of his bed still biting at his pencil.

"Don't get it," he said aloud, shaking his head at George Raft on the wall. "Got the wrong stupid speed, or something. I'll definitely 'ave to get a tape recorder tomorrow..." And with a sudden show of anger he lifted a pillow and punched into it, hard, against a wall. "Else it's Paki stuff!" he said, looking as if he wanted to spit.

Some miles away Narinder was nervously opening the door at the head of the printing shop stairs. After that sudden decision in the garden, the final making-up of her mind, and then a couldn't-care-less feeling which had seen her through the getting ready – in the shower, at the mirror, putting on her disco clothes – Narinder was trying to get out. But her defiance and her cool had suddenly deserted her. In her school uniform in the garden she'd been the rebel – stop me if you can. Now, looking the woman, she felt like a little kid. All right, she looked great: but that was going to be no good getting her past her dad. It was one of the things that would stop her.

Pratap was busy cleaning one of the hand presses, rubbing hard at a roller with a white spirit cloth. He hadn't looked up yet, and Narinder, at the foot of the stairs, thought for a crazy moment that she might make it. She put a sudden lightness into her step and tried to skip past him while his head was down. "Just popping round to Paula's," she said, "won't be long."

But there was never any skipping past her father: she might have known that: did know it. His head came up quicker than a watch-dog's. "Stop, Narinder!" His eyes focused, he looked her up and down, frowning, waved at her with the cloth. "What's all this, please?"

So, the first go had failed. Well, she'd known this wasn't going to be easy, hadn't she? She tried the bluff, kept her voice high and unstressed as she went to move on. "Mum said it's O.K. with her as long as – " But she didn't get another step.

"Mum said what is O.K. with her?" Her father came round the counter, and all at once she stopped feeling nervous, because now she had nothing to be nervous about. He just wasn't going to let her go. All the same, she struggled on, along the path she'd started. "I'm only going round Paula's. Not gonna be long."

She stared him out – and suddenly her father made her jump as he threw the cloth to the floor in a rare display of temper. "What have you been saying to this girl?" he shouted up the stairs towards Kamal: and just as suddenly softening, he turned to Narinder, smiled weakly, explained to her with his hands stroking downwards at his beard. "Nindy, you know I can't let you go out at night on your own. And you know why, as well. But please remember it is only for your own protection. Now go upstairs again. Watch the telly, read your books, telephone Paula to come round here. But I'm sorry ..."

Defiance, nervousness, calm – and now a choking surge of anger: she'd been through it all and suddenly she wanted to scream, even to hit him. Did he know what he looked like, her father, pawing at his face, shaping the air with his scared hands, keeping her in because he hadn't got the guts to go to the police? It made her mad, his whole frightened attitude. "Oh, yeah," she sneered in a voice she'd never used to him before, "so Paula can run the risk of going out at night, but I can't?"

"You saw that man!" His hands were still desperately trying to explain. "She is not running your risk."

But her hands had gone hot, she was clenching and stretching them in her anger. "But it's *stupid*!" She turned, walked a pace, came back. "I'm fourteen years of age! You can't keep me locked up here like a prisoner! Not even you!"

She thought he was going to slap her, but to her surprise his voice stayed very calm and reasonable. "Nobody's home is a prison, Narinder," he tried to tell her.

But she'd gone past any time for being told. "Oh, I don't care!" she shouted at him. "Listen, what sort of life is this, anyway?" She heard the screech in her voice. "I might as well be dead the way you're going on!"

"Narinder, you're my daughter and this is for your own good. It's for your safety."

Her eyes gazed at him. That face again! That give-up face! "Oh, come on! How's anyone gonna get me round at Paula's?" In that instant she even believed she was going there herself. "It's all bluff – they've got you going, that lot. What you've got to do is report 'em – not lock up your own daughter like this was Holloway!"

But still he persisted, the same even tone as if he were reading from the Granth. "These are dangerous people..."

"Oh, yeah? An' why? Only 'cos you let them be!" And now it came out in tears. She was at the end of everything – no life here to look forward to, no friend any more to look forward to it with, and the only thing going for the five minutes she'd got left before they shot her off to India was Tommy, a bit of fun, a laugh for a couple of hours to forget all *this*. Now she found herself standing her ground and shouting as if she were someone else. "I'm going round Paula's," she yelled, and she ran for the shop door. "I'll be back ten o'clock. An' if you want to stop me, you've got to do it with your own two hands!"

Through her outrage she saw her father looking at his oily fingers: across her shoulders she felt the cleanness of her disco top. And in her head she was telling herself she was fourteen. He hadn't laid a hand on her in over four years.

"Narinder! I'm your father and I'm telling you..." He stepped round a bale of paper, took a pace towards her.

"No!" She bent to a bolt. "Forget telling! You gotta stop me!" And almost as if she were in a trance she slid one bolt and started reaching for the others. Her shoulders tingled, they

93

ached, waiting for the grab of her father's hands. As she started to turn the handle of the door he came up behind her, he wiped a hand on his handkerchief, lifted it – and with a flick of his wrist to shake down his steel kara he took a look at his watch.

"Half past nine," he said.

"Quarter to ten." She opened the door wider and stepped out.

He came behind her to look up and down the street – which is when she kissed him, and thanked him, in Punjabi, before running off fast along the pavement.

eight

Over at Frank's the air was sharp with family quarrelling. Nothing wounds quite like the needle teeth of a domestic dispute. Mick said he preferred to stand, so Ellie stood to match him and Frank was left trying to lounge back and play the whole thing down. Dolly, at her own request, had stayed at home with the kids.

"At least half a dozen of Frank's people could've been monkeying about with Dolly's handbag," Ellie was saying. "Aren't you jumping to things a bit, Michael?"

Mick didn't bat an eye. "You have to jump to get across some things, Ellie. Which ain't saying it's easy. But Brian was up Paula's school today, asking her whether I was in or out – and when I get in I find Dad's musical box has gone."

Ellie puffed rapidly at a cigarette, like an old movie actress in a big scene. "So on the strength of that you're accusing him of being a thief! What about those people who turned your house over before? Are you saying it's our Brian in front of one of them?"

Every so often Mick and Ellie had their differences, but never anything as personal as this. Frank got up, made a profound sucking noise, tried to smooth things over. "All right, Mick, there's only one way. If it'll satisfy you, since you're family, we'll let you ask him, ask the boy. That should give you your answer – then you can go chasing the others. Now, will that do?"

Whether it would or would not, it still didn't suit Ellie. "Or perhaps you've brought a search warrant!" She thrust her face at Mick, withdrew it with a wobble.

"Don't be like that, Ellie. No, that'll do me, Frank. Let's just see his face. I can read a lot in a face."

"Seems to me you can read a lot into a lot of things!" Ellie told him. "But come on then, let's go through your panto-mime ..."

Up in his bedroom Brian was pumping iron. A large Union Jack towel was draped over his weight-lifting bench, and his face was almost as red as the crosses of St. George and St. Patrick as he lifted twenty-five kilos vertically above his chest.

Frank rapped at the door loudly and went in. "It's only me and Uncle Micky."

But it was Ellie, too. She pushed past the men and stood looking down at the sweating Brian as he manoeuvred the weights out of the way with a thud. "Bri, he's only got some stupid story about you getting into his house and making off with that musical box!"

"Do what?" Brian's grin, his outraged innocence and mild amusement would have done justice to one of the film star posters on the wall. "Here, what is this, *Disney-time*?"

Mick, though, still hadn't batted an eye. "Just a straight yes or no, son. Clear it all up. Did you have a key off my Doll and go round my house today?"

Brian smirked. "No, 'course not. Why should I?" He went to wipe himself down, but contented himself with a bend to the flag to rub at his face.

"But you were up Paula's school dinner-time, weren't you?" Mick persisted. "You ain't making my Paula out a liar?"

" 'Course I'm not. I saw her from the street. 'Blimey, Mick, she is my cousin. Just said hello, that's all. Asked after you, that sort of thing. She must've got it all wrong in her 'ead."

Mick stared. Frank coughed. Ellie snorted and wanted to go, turned to Mick: but he didn't budge.

"All right," Brian volunteered. "Where you wanna look?" With a big show of the man with nothing to hide, rapidly he lifted his mattress, opened drawers, swept curtains aside, invited a look under the divan. Mick looked carefully in all those places. "Come on, where is it, then?"

"All right, Bri, thanks," Frank said.

"Satisfied?" Ellie crowed at Mick.

He nodded slowly. "Well, yeah . . . " But he had a last flip of the duvet, all the same. "Yeah, all right, I'm satisfied. I'm sorry. I'm very sorry." He shook Frank's hand, then Brian's, but by the time he turned to Ellie she'd gone, thumped down the thickly carpeted stairs. "But I'm still bloomin' puzzled, I tell you."

Shaking his head, Mick followed Frank down, said an awkward goodbye in the porch: while upstairs, behind the closed door, Brian watched for him to go, then carefully adjusted the towel on the bench to make sure that nothing of what was hidden beneath it could show.

Certain adjustments were being made elsewhere as well; but back in Shepherd's Gate these were mental adjustments, character opinions being revised as Narinder began to discover things about the out-of-school Tommy Parsons, the boy who was a kid around the playground, and the big man in the evening.

For a start, he wasn't waiting outside the *Denmark Arms*, he was inside it, leaning back against a pillar and chatting-up the middle-aged barmaid like a regular. And what he was wearing made him look ten years older – the loose-fitting jacket with the sleeves pushed up, the baggy trousers, the expensive shirt. Narinder, although she was dressed-up herself, just about dared to put her head round the door, tried to attract his attention in an uncertain voice. "Tommy!"

Tommy turned, played it cool, didn't let on he'd seen her. But "Gotta go," he said, with a flick of his head in Narinder's direction, and out he walked like someone bored by all this female attention. A surge of anger welled up in Narinder. Who did this jerk think he was? She'd really upset her father, forced him down to his knees, so that she could come out tonight. And with *this*?

"Where d'you wanna go?" he asked her, flicking his collar, not a word about how good she looked.

"I thought we was going to the disco. That's what you said."

"Yeah, all right, then." And he walked her along the Barking Road, with an arm casually slung round her shoulder, a dangling hand a bit too close. What had she got into? Narinder asked herself. This wasn't what she'd reckoned, this 'big deal' big-head on an ego trip. She'd been surprised, caught out: and while she didn't mind going along with it for a bit, just for fun, she really wouldn't have minded being back at home with her parents. Until Tommy said those magic words. "One in the eye for Prescott, eh, Nind?" And then she smiled, relaxed a bit and unwound Tommy's arm to hold his hand safely at her side. All right, this was what growing up in London was all about, wasn't it? So the least she could do was enjoy it while she could and pity a certain person who was missing out.

But even at that moment Pratap was checking on her, ringing Paula's mother to make sure that she was safely there. The answer he got, though, was the one that parents dread. She hadn't been seen. What was more, she wasn't expected – and it was now well after any time she might have arrived.

A worried Punjabi oath slipped out. "I'll be coming round, O.K.? Straightaway. I must talk to your Paula, please." And before Dolly could object, could explain that they were in some sort of a crisis themselves, the phone was hung up and Pratap was shouting up the stairs to tell Kamal where he was going.

At the Wakefield Centre Tommy became someone else again: someone between the two people Narinder had seen so far. Here he was known, and he couldn't quite play the man. But he wasn't Jack-the-lad of the school and the bus top, either. Here he smiled more, attempted to please, showed the bulge of his cigarettes rather than taking one out and lighting it.

A community centre, the Wakefield had all the disco atmosphere of a London Underground ticket hall. Play-group paintings in thick splodges were taped crookedly to the walls, the lights were too bright, and there were too many tables and chairs. Coke and sandwiches were being served from a noisy kitchen hatch, while the only person the music seemed to please was the D.J., who looked young enough to be a mate of Dean's.

As soon as they got in Narinder took a quick look round to sort the racial mix: nothing conscious, but something she always did as one of the ethnic minority. Although it was International Night they were nearly all white, just a couple of groups of Caribbeans: and she was definitely the only one from an Asian family. Not surprising. Even after all these years it still took a bit of face to break out of the gurdwara circle. And although the whites who were there didn't act skinhead she was still on her own to start with because Tommy had seen a table of mates and just went over to them.

Well, she decided, she wasn't going to trot after him! She wasn't some sort of pet on a lead. She could stand on her own two feet without any help from Tommy, thank you very much. She'd get herself a Coke. And if he didn't come back quick she'd clear off home before someone told Prescott how much notice he'd taken of her.

Dean, for the second time in recent weeks, had found something more interesting than the telly going on in his living room. Nothing as frightening as the night the raiders had come, but dramatic enough for him to keep the sound turned well down while the talk went on, staring at the Sikh in his turban sitting on their settee.

"Paula," the man was saying, "I want you to tell me

anything you know, please. Anything. Now, why would she be telling me she was coming round to you?"

Paula shook her head. She was up to there with Narinder, but she still wouldn't drop her in it with her dad. You didn't hurt people who were sick. "I dunno," she struggled.

"It's getting very serious, you see."

Mr Sidhu was well upset, she could tell, stroking down his beard with both hands.

"Nearly an hour to go a five-minute journey. That's not right." He turned to look at her mother, suddenly stiffened. "She's missing. My Narinder is a missing person!" The words of it somehow made everything seem worse.

"You'll have to tell the police, Mr Sidhu."

"Yes. But there is my cleft stick." Pratap stood up, buttoned his coat with swift fingers. "These people, who knows what they might do if I go to the police?"

Dean rolled his eyes. "Who knows what they've done already?"

"Dean! What people, Mr Sidhu?" Paula's mother asked. "Are you saying someone's done something to Narinder – someone you know?"

Paula sat and listened, forced her mouth shut tight. Even with Nindy's dad so upset, she still couldn't just out and tell him where she was, could she? "*Look down the Wakefield! Ask for a boy called Tommy Parsons!*" She couldn't come out with anything like that or Nindy's feet wouldn't touch the ground!

But before Mr Sidhu could get to the door, her own father had come in, drawn a blank at Brian's by the look on his face. In a mood, he threw himself down into an armchair and listened with bare patience to what Dolly was telling him about Narinder.

"She was all dressed up," she explained. "She told her dad she was coming round here to see Paula."

"You two got something going on?" Mick asked.

"No, Dad, honest. Straight up."

"Straight up!" Dean was like a roused dog.

And Mick's blue eyes were boring into Paula, drawing out the colour in her cheeks and in her neck. "I can read a face, Paula Prescott," he told her. "I can round here at any rate. So what's goin' on, eh? 'Ave you just had me making a fool of myself over Ilford?"

Paula's first thought was to splutter; then to cry; then to run and slam out of the room. And why not? She'd every right. She'd done nothing, had she, and here was all the world turning on her! But any of that would only make them think the worst, she told herself: so she tried to answer all their stares by carefully telling them what she safely felt she could.

"Dad, it's nothing terrible like Mr Sidhu thinks it is, honest. An' nothing to do with me, or you going over Ilford. What Nindy's done's off her own bat. But she's all right. There's nothing *up*." She looked from one to another of their disbelieving stares. "It's just I can't tell you, that's all."

But she had broken the seal. The secret wasn't airtight any longer. And Mr Sidhu, knowing now that there was more Paula could tell him, was shaking a finger at her. "Listen, please: my daughter goes out all dressed up, she tells me lies about where she's going, she dares me to stop her by force – yes, when there are wicked people about who threaten her with harm – and you can tell me there is nothing wrong?" His eyes were filling with tears: anger now and frustration. He *had* to know where his daughter was, his face said, or he'd burst.

But Mick had folded his arms, was suddenly very interested. "Here, what wicked people are these?" he asked, first at Pratap, then at Paula.

"Protection people," the Indian told him. "Elkin's gang, you know. Sends a man who despoils my shop with black ink, threatens our lives ..."

"*Black ink?*" Mick frowned.

"Oh, ink is nothing, you see. You can wash ink off after a

time, buy new bottles. But not blood! You can't get rid of the stain of blood, or buy new bottles for your daughter!"

And that was what did it, Paula reckoned: the talk about daughters and spilt blood. "I ain't asking you, girl, I'm telling!" her dad shouted. "You tell this gentleman where your mate is, and quick about it. If you know where she's gone, you put the poor bloke's mind at rest right now, you hear me?"

Dolly closed her eyes at his shouting: but he'd made himself clear enough, to Paula and Nindy's father, probably the street. And, sinking back in the settee, picking at her fingers, Paula hesitantly began telling them what had happened between her and Narinder.

"We had this row. Something about our Brian – I still don't get it. Called him a crook, she did, and us! All crooks! Real bust-up, we've had…"

Mick looked at Dolly, pursed his lips as if clamming on some secret thought of his own.

"… Then on the bus home Tommy Parsons asked her out to a disco, International Night. And she was still all in a huff – didn't know where she was – so she said yes. Sort of, 'I'll show *her*!' You know…" Paula stopped: suddenly felt sick inside at what she'd just said, at what she'd given away. "There! Now I've shown *her*, an' that weren't what I wanted." She sighed and looked down at the carpet. "She'll kill me for telling."

Mick jerked his head, the boxer. "'S'all right, girl, I'd have killed you if you hadn't."

Pratap was halfway out of the door. "Where is this … this disco?" he asked.

"Down the Wakefield; Church Army. But please don't…" All at once Paula felt as if she'd just personally delivered Nindy to the airport.

"I'll give you a run down in the cab."

"It's all right, I have my own car. Just tell me where to go…" He was shaking his car keys impatiently.

"The girl'll take you. Paula can show you the way," Mick

offered. "'Cos we ain't crooks, mate, an' we won't never be
.."

Paula took in a deep breath. Not only not crooks, but too blessed honest – her dad was only asking her to be brave about the insults and face Nindy out with the truth of what she'd had to say to the man.

"This family stands by everything it does."

And that gave Paula the courage: but it was still very reluctantly that she went. Sitting next to the man in the car and directing him to where he could catch Nindy out with Tommy definitely didn't seem the sort of thing that could make things all right between them – no matter what it proved to Mr Sidhu.

Inside, Tommy had found his way back to Narinder, was suddenly acting as if he were glad she was there after all. The music being played had turned slow and Tommy had decided to get close, holding Narinder so tight it made it hard for her to breath.

"I'll really remember tonight," she told him, "if I live."

Tommy loosened his hold a bit. "Don't know me own strength, that's my trouble..."

Narinder looked around her at all the cuddling. "I never should've come."

For which she got a bigger squeeze. "Go on, it's hardly started, give it a chance." His voice went into his throat. "Gonna be a great night for you an' me ..." He pushed himself close again.

"Not if you crack a rib it won't!"

"It's s'posed to be a smoocher." As if to prove his point. Tommy rubbed his cheek against Narinder's, ran a hand down her spine as if he were God's gift to women.

From the doorway Pratap saw only the general scene at first, his eyes trying to adjust to the light which someone had turned out: but before he saw more Narinder broke free.

"I came for a dance, not all that!" she told Tommy, and sat herself down on a chair.

"Please yourself! Oi, wotcha, Wendy..." Immediately, Tommy had turned to someone else.

But by now, Pratap's vision had sorted itself enough and he had skirted the floor to come up behind his daughter. Angrily, he poked her on the shoulder.

"Dad!" The word came out in a gasp, but it took Narinder several seconds to work out actually who he was. Of course she knew her own father: but the sight of him where she'd never expected to see him threw her completely. Not that anything threw Tommy. He neatly danced Wendy well away from the aggravation.

"Don't say a single word!" Pratap grabbed his daughter by the wrist. And Narinder, still struck dumb, went where he pulled her, out through the pairs of cuddling dancers and into the street. Her mind was still racing, though, trying to get things sorted into some sensible shape. How had this happened? What was it that had brought her father chasing round the Wakefield?

The second she saw the car she knew. Like thinking of someone's name that had escaped her, when the answer came it seemed so obvious: why the hell hadn't she thought of it straight off? What could have been more bloody obvious than Paula, looking out from the car window, all smug.

"Prescott!" Narinder exploded. "Should'a known, shouldn't I?" For a second she pulled at her father's arm and threatened to walk away, but it was from Paula Prescott, not from him. She wanted to shake her fist, swear, do all sorts of dramatic things. Telling Prescott what she was would have helped relieve her feelings. But why give her the satisfaction of that, she thought. So she slammed herself into the front passenger seat and said nothing: did up her safety belt with a hefty click and stared straight ahead out of the windscreen.

She heard Paula clear her throat: make that little noise she always did before she said something serious.

"I wouldn't have done it for the world, Nind. Honest. They forced me to tell 'em. He thought you'd been kidnapped, your dad. He was goin' spare!"

Gripped tight in his own tension Narinder's father was concentrating on the road as if he were on his driving test, leaning forward in the way he always did when he was worried. "Narinder, I trusted you, and you told me lies," he suddenly said to the windscreen. "You tell me Paula's and then you come to a dance-hall. What will it be the next time, eh? On the Underground to the West End, is it?" There wasn't much she could say: she *had* told him a lie. He'd just found her out, that was all, thanks to Prescott. "No," he said, still concentrating very hard and yet going over a red light, "I'm getting you back to India quicker than lightning, I'm telling you."

Narinder slumped back. Exactly what she'd expected him to say: but this had still been like blowing all your pocket money on one big treat, and the treat turns out a flop. Except this was a million times worse. Not even a fair time tonight to remember – and now everything was over. Now all she had to look forward to was that new life thousands of miles away with a grandmother she didn't even know watching over her like a hawk.

But Paula was sitting forward. In the middle of all her depressing thoughts Narinder was suddenly aware of the girl going on strong into her father's ear, the way she could when she really wanted to sell you on something. "Oh, come on, Mr Sidhu, I'm telling you it was only on account of me. We had this fall-out and then she went and done that on the rebound. You've done that, haven't you?" But her father said nothing and Paula sat back with a sigh. Then suddenly she was up and leaning forward again. "Besides, there's nothing wrong with a disco, you know, not up them places. There's never any drinking or smoking or drugs, they're all run proper. I tell you, my dad lets me go." There was still no response, just that hard stare out at the road. Now Paula's voice went high, almost sarcastic. "Don't boys and girls ever meet one another over India, then?" She leant over from the back and put an arm around Narinder. "Anyhow, I know Nindy, she's my best mate, and she's straight as a die, you take it from me ..." And Narinder, wanting to snort at such a pathetic attempt to make up to her found that she couldn't: and, worse, she suddenly didn't want to shrug the arm away either.

Which at least somehow got them talking, so that in her bedroom ten minutes later, while her father was going on to her mother in the kitchen, she and Paula had it out, straight. The girl had insisted on coming up, practically foot-in-the-door stuff, and now, staring at her and looking as miserable as she felt, Paula came out with it, demanded a clear answer.

"Come on, then, Nind. What is this about my cousin and me being crooks? What're you on about? Eh? Only I'd like to know, like – 'cos I'm not ..." Her arms were folded, her weight unbalanced, one foot tapping nervously on the floor.

Narinder tried to keep it straight, knew she couldn't just shout an abusive answer to this any more: knew in her bones that Paula hadn't *had* to come and face her out, could've run off home after showing her dad to the Wakefield if she'd wanted to. So, with a little look at Guru Nanak on the wall, finding a sort of calmness from somewhere, she sat Paula down, spread her own hands out flat as if the story were there to be read, printed on the pages of her palms, and told her in as matter-of-fact tone as she could, that the man who had gone to the school, Paula's cousin, had been the man she'd told her about. The protection collector. But she couldn't help her voice rising a bit. "He's only the one who comes here, who's helping get me sent over India, that's all! Don't you see? He's the one threatening my dad, who spilt that ink, got him all scared about me ..."

Paula screwed up her eyes, shook her head, a lack of understanding more than disbelief. "Are you sure, Narinder?"

"You don't forget them hate eyes in a hurry. An' I can still hear his slimy voice: 'Mr Elkin hates hurting kids'! *Mr Elkin!* You do know who *he* is?" Suddenly all Narinder wanted Paula to know was the depth her cousin had sunk to.

"Elkin! Nind, my gr – ..." Paula's quick reaction had slipped out. She even put her hand over her mouth, but it didn't hide her eyes, and there some light had dawned...

"Eh?" Narinder pressed. She was right on the edge of knowing something.

Now Paula was back to staring at her feet. "All right, it weren't no crime, but my grandad had a to-do with that Elkin. You know, after that hold-up." She looked up, definitely as if she was deciding what she should say. "An' I know he's nicked my musical box, that Brian." It still made no sense, but it sounded as if she was trying to come as clean as she could, unwrapping a bit of family secret. "*That's* what he was up the school about this morning. Making sure my dad was out..."

"Your musical box?" It did sound like some stupid fairy-tale. "What's he want that for?"

"Not to sit and play the tunes, I can tell you." Paula looked at the door, sat close, took a deep breath. "Listen, Nind, it's all to do with that Elkin and my grandad. You putting Brian in with him – I get it now, it makes a bit of sense." The girl looked the way she did when an algebra equation worked out to something like an answer. She dropped her voice. "If Brian's in with Elkin, and Brian's took my musical box, I reckon I know where Grandad hid..." Her eyes were wide. "Nindy, there's a special message in that musical box. Meant for me. Only no-one else is supposed to know about it, especially Elkin..."

Narinder shivered. "Eh?" It was all very frightening, even bigger than the cousin coming in with his threats, if Paula was talking about Elkin as if she'd got some secret on him. After what she'd thought about Paula's family, this was *really* icy.

"Nind – will you help me get my musical box back off him?"

"What, off Brian?" This was all really confusing – and moving so fast. . .

"I've got to get it back now!" That light was even brighter in Paula's eyes. We can do it tomorrow, when they're down the car sales. Auntie Ellie always does her shopping Saturday mornings – and I reckon I know a way in. . ."

"Hang on." Narinder's hands tried to calm her, while in her throat she did some very quick swallowing: because before they were a minute older, the two of them, she'd got to have the answer to a question. A very important question.

"Is it . . . this getting it back . . . is it . . . ?" But it was not so easy to ask. "Is it *against* Elkin, then? Doing him down? Or just some family fight?" There, it was out. But she had to know. It was only fair, and it would put things very straight between them.

"It's definitely not *for* him," Paula replied. "If I get that back at least I'll know what Grandad wanted me to know – and that won't help Elkin, I can tell you!" There was a new fight in her, a determination which somehow needed matching. And almost against herself, Narinder found that she very much wanted to be in on this – like everyone doing something they shouldn't do at school, a sort of hysteria. And she was thinking how Saturday morning was when her dad always had a lot of running about to do, to the cash-and-carry for the paper bags he printed on, and delivering . . . So that all at once she felt that same do-or-die choking in her throat again, the one she'd had earlier, going out. Why not, then? She'd been quick enough to call her best mate a criminal; so didn't she owe her a favour now?

"All right! Give it a go!"

"Great! Good old Nind!" Paula gave her a strong hug, almost as bad as Tommy Parsons. Narinder felt very good, seeing the pleasure in her old friend's eyes. And she knew there was a definite gleam in her own as well: because the thought had suddenly struck her that she might have a slim chance now to get a bit of her own back against the people who were driving her away. And that was something she'd never forgive herself for turning down.

nine

Saturday morning meant early starts all round. Paula was up and dressed while Dolly swallowed a quick breakfast; Pratap was up and starting his hatch-back; Brian was up and giving a story to Frank about going in late to work so that he could look over a second-hand motor out at Gidea Park. And they were all on secret errands of their own, all doing something they wouldn't want advertised: one taking the deeds of his business to a man who could get Air India tickets; one keen to get out and buy a simple cassette recorder he could use in his own room; one getting permission to take her pocket money out of her mother's handbag, but fumbling for a small set of keys which had been kept in a pocket at the back ever since her Grandad had gone to Ilford.

Narinder was waiting for Paula by the bus stop, grateful that Kamal had swallowed a story about getting a library book she needed for her homework. With the sun shining so bright in all the corners it hadn't been nearly as hard as she'd thought, as if, after all the shouting and the tears, she could never dream of telling a lie again in a million years. But when she saw Paula pull the keys out of her pocket she knew it wasn't the same sort of stunt they were on at all. This was much, much worse: police station stuff, if they were caught.

"Mum still had these, from when Grandad was there – you know, emergency."

"I'll say emergency! You sure they won't be in?" Narinder's hand was holding tight to the bus stop. How far down the list from protection was burglary?

"Shouldn't be, not if they're acting normal. But we'll keep our eyes skinned for a bit . . ."

On the timing they'd made a good start, didn't have to wait long for a bus, which meant that the Ilford end of things had to be delayed. But they found a handy alley between gardens on the other side of the road from Frank's house where they could hide and check that the drive was free of cars – and spot any movement inside through the big picture window. So, anxiously they waited, hoping no-one would ask them what they were doing, Narinder's eyes up and down the street, Paula's on the flitting figure in the house. And at last, after a good twenty minutes, Ellie came out, all dressed to the nines and a Harrods' bag, to go shopping up the High Street.

They gave it longer yet, they had to be sure. But when the moment did come it was as if there was an invisible tape stretched across their path. After all, Paula was family: and whatever her reasons for doing this, she was still breaking into her own Uncle Frank's: while Narinder still felt fixed by thoughts of her father's anger if she were charged with burglary. So it was all very mixed up, and difficult to take the first step.

In the end it was Narinder who got them moving. "Come on," she said, "I didn't come here for no sun tan." Putting down the people who scared her father had to be worth some risk. And out she stepped, looked both ways, and marched across the road. Bold as brass, as Dolly would have said. Up the drive to the front door just as if they were doing no more than making a friendly family call; a big act. And without looking round, fingers trembling, steeling themselves to behave as if all this were above-board, one put the Chubb Key in and the other the Yale, to save time; so that within seconds of crossing the road Paula was in the kitchen and neutralizing the burglar alarm the way the family did, using the third key on the ring.

Paula reckoned she'd learned something about searching a house. She could remember the first places Elkin's men had gone for when they'd turned her place over; she also reckoned her Uncle Frank and Auntie Ellie wouldn't have the first idea what Brian was into. "It's not downstairs, I'm sure of that," she whispered. She headed for the stairs. "We 'aven't got to search all over. It's in his bedroom, got to be ..."

Narinder went up with her, tried not to think about them cutting themselves off from their only way of escape. Perhaps if she'd seen Brian's car coming back through the Saturday morning traffic, a cassette recorder in a bag on one of the seats, she'd have acted a bit less bold. But in they went without a backward glance to Brian's tip of a bedroom.

"Bed first," Paula commanded as if she knew. She lifted the mattress, pulled the divan out to see if the base had got something up inside it while Narinder pulled up the pillows, wrinkling her nose at the dirty hankie which came with it. But what was underneath was a much more welcome find: not that she knew it at first. "Tell he's a crook!" she told Paula. "Look here! You wouldn't get up very quick after being hit with this, would you?"

Paula came out from under the base and looked across, saw what Narinder was pointing at lying deep in the ruck of Brian's sheets: the cylinder out of her grandad's musical box. "That's a bit of it!" she hissed. "That's the roller thing! He *does* know – he's stripped it down already!"

Frantically they searched on, under the divan again, in the wardrobe, dragged the weight-lifting bench over to look on its top: and as they did, the Union Jack towel slipped from it – and left the musical box dusty but very exposed against the white paint of the skirting board.

"Got it! Great, Nind!" Practically diving on it Paula opened the lid. Narinder stared, expecting to see the gutted inside: instead of which, what they both saw was the mechanism complete, just a duller look to the substitute cyclinder.

"Would you...? It's still got a roller in it! Look!"

But suddenly there wasn't a second to look at anything; because what they both heard, very loud and very close, was the slam of a car door immediately under the window, followed by the crunch of hard boots on the gravel.

Narinder caught her breath, leaned over to look – and just about stifled her scream. "He's here! *Him!*" She started pushing Paula for the door. "Quick! He's here!"

Desperate to be quick but fumbling, tripping over each other and the bench and the bedding, they slid the musical box and the old cyclinder into their strong shopping bag and scurried for the stairs. With a bit of luck, if he was getting anything out of his boot, they'd just about make it down the stairs and round to the kitchen before he came in through the front door.

But Brian wasn't getting anything out of his boot. He'd got what he wanted in his hand, had swung straight out of the car with it. So Paula and Narinder were only halfway down the stairs when he came into the hall with the cassette recorder and caught the pair of them frozen there with the shopping bag between them.

Instinctively, Brian dropped what he was carrying onto the cushion of the telephone seat, and took the hands-by-sides fighting stance all the hard men used. "Oh, yeah?" he said. "Oh, yeah! What's all this then? Come looking for suthing, 'ave you?" He flexed his shoulders and took a step nearer, staring all the while at Paula.

"It's mine!" she said defiantly. "You didn't have no right ..."

"Right? *Right?*" Brian looked away and back, sneering. "He was my grandad an' all, you know. He died here, remember? I played him that more'n you, that last week. Just ... left suthing in it, that's all. Got a right to get it back, if we're talking about rights ..." He took another step nearer to them. "Now just you put that down on the stair an' get out! Right?" He looked very threatening, with the gangland face of violence his family had never seen. But Narinder had: and she knew only too well that he'd do anything, cousin or not, to stop Paula taking the musical box away.

"Why should I?" Paula was demanding. "It's not yours, it's mine."

"*Put it down!*" Then Brian tried a casual half-gesture with one hand, quietened his voice. "You'll get it back, kid, I promise you . . . "

"Oh, yeah, when?"

"Listen, I don't *wanna* have to get rough. Now just put it down, eh?" He even tried a family smile.

At which Paula dropped her shoulders, sighed, and moved slowly down the stairs with heavy feet. "Oh, all right. But you let me have it back soon, all right?"

"I said, didn't I?" Brian relaxed and came forward with a hand held out – when suddenly, with a surprising violence Paula swung the heavy bag back and brought it forward quick and hard to go thudding into his groin.

"Oooof!" His eyes went wide and he looked as if he were imitating a goldfish.

"Quick! Out the back!" Paula yelled. She rounded the banister post. Narinder vaulted over. The pain and the surprise gave them a vital five seconds before Brian, clutching at himself, his eyes filled with tears, swore the paint off the woodwork and came hobbling after them. They ran for the kitchen, slammed the door on him. But the Banham keys, still in their locks on the back door, were a fumble one-handed, and, "*Give it here!*" – Brian was into the kitchen already. "You can't get out! Give it here!" He was only a grab away from Narinder. Desperately, her eyes swept the kitchen for something to throw: but the surfaces were all clear, except for . . .

"Quick!" she screeched at Paula. Brian was standing tight behind the other door, drawing in his breath, knowing he'd got them. She picked up the only thing, a plastic bottle of cooking oil, and threw it with all the force she could at his feet.

With a *plop* it burst its seam on the quarry tiles. Oil splattered Brian's shoes and quickly spread a thick, slippery barrier between him and the girls.

"You stupid ..." Lurching forward, he tried to step over it before it ran too far, but he'd already got it on his heel, and with a twist his foot shot forward from under him and he fell heavily into the worst of it.

Paula had got the door open. "Come on!"

The more Brian struggled to get up, the more he spread the Mazola, onto his palms and his elbows. He laid his mouth to all the obscenities ever invented, threatened things to curl the hair. But a couple of words from Narinder were a hundred times more telling.

"Sorry it weren't black ink, *big man*!" she sneered. And they both ran, weren't within earshot to hear Brian's perverted reply to that.

It might have been heavy, but they carried the musical box back from the bus stop in triumph, tight smiles of success in the serious circumstances. Narinder looked at the watch on her free arm. She reckoned she could count on another half-hour before she had to be back – just time enough to inspect what they'd got up in Paula's bedroom.

"But how you going to tell your dad you got it?"

Paula stopped while they changed hands, swapped positions on the pavement. "I'll just tell him. It's mine, isn't it? Why should I feel bad?"

Away from the excitement of what they'd done the seriousness seemed to grow. "What about the floor?" But Narinder already knew the answer. Who cared about that scum's kitchen floor?

"Can't wait to hear this new roller," Paula was saying. "He definitely made it for a reason ..."

"What, him?"

"No, Grandad. Grandad made that, out in his shed. Had a load of these bars of stuff." Paula stopped, rubbed her hands again. "But what's it trying to say? That's what I want to know ..."

Back in Paula's bedroom they wound the mechanism and were listening to it almost before the door closed behind them. But what that narrow band of raised spikes round the middle of the cylinder was trying to say was too deep a mystery. It wasn't anything like a tune either of them knew.

"It's saying something – it's some message, an' I know it's for me," Paula said after they'd heard it through three times. "But it's like some foreign language when you haven't got the dictionary ..."

Narinder, her eye very much on the time now, shook her head. "That's a rotten shame, that is." And really disappointing, she thought, because after all that business out at Ilford, she'd definitely hoped it might have been some sort of a help to her.

"See, it's definitely a code. He said it would be." Paula went on looking, in the lid, ran her fingers underneath the walnut case. "Only trouble is, he never gave me the key."

Which left Narinder up in the air, and with no other option than to suddenly mumble, "See you!" and run back fast to her own house.

By two o'clock on the Saturday Frank was on his own in the showroom. Dolly had cleared her desk and the workshop was shut. Of Brian there'd been no sign, but Frank wouldn't be all that long himself; it was just that on Saturdays when West Ham were playing away it was sometimes worth hanging on till the lunchtime pubs turned out. Impulse buying, especially after a few drinks, had always been a part of the way the East End got new things and a signature on an agreement was rarely argued over afterwards. People only do drunk what they'd like to do sober.

As he watched two men come in, hard-looking, the sort who sometimes wanted a car to work a con, he pressed a new, lower price on the Daimler in the window, counted the nine's to make sure he wasn't giving a silly bargain away. One of them came over to it, looked at his own reflection in the bonnet, stepped back, kicked a wheel.

"Frank Butler?" the other one said.

"That's right, in person. Looking for something special or you just here for kicks?"

"Funny man!" Ron Martin, who'd kicked the tyre, put his hands in his pockets and sauntered round to Frank. "You can shut up shop, son, that's what you can do."

"I beg your pardon?"

Barrett started switching off showroom lights. "You heard, Frank. Lock this place up and come with us."

No-one in any way of business in the East End is totally surprised by a visit from the boys, because everyone knows where they stand in the eyes of people like Elkin. Everyone's got a place in the network. You might get left alone because someone's cousin once did someone a favour, or you pay straight protection, or you do some other sort of deal. And these were the facts of life: they didn't make you a criminal, but they did keep things nice and sweet. Which makes it all the more of a surprise when the muscle suddenly walks in and cuts up rough.

Frank stood his ground for one more question. "Who says?" he asked. But he really didn't need to be told.

"You'll see."

Charlie Elkin's Mercedes was parked in a quiet lay-by in Epping Forest: no sign of a driver, just the track-suited man himself, towel at his neck, sitting in the back with a grapefruit juice and that morning's *Mirror*. Barrett ushered the car dealer out of the motor they'd brought him in. "He's waiting for you," he told him. And "Frank Butler," he announced to the gold rims bent over the crossword.

"Know anything about girls' games?" Elkin asked, as Frank got in and sat uncomfortably next to him, stared at the king of the East End himself. "Seven letter word – 'in the firing line at netball'. Any ideas?"

As frightened as he looked, Frank still tried to keep his end up. "Mr Elkin, you didn't make me shut up my business to get your crossword done."

Elkin looked up from the paper and stared at Frank; cold, dead eyes that said he'd be the judge of that. "No, you're right," he agreed in a flat voice. "It's your boy, Frank. Or should I say, our boy. He's the reason. Our Brian ..." The frown on Frank's face looked very genuine. "Hasn't he ever told you who he works for?"

"Why should he? He works for me. He's a junior partner in the family business."

"Oh, no." Elkin glanced back at his crossword, ticked off a clue number with his expensive gold ballpoint. "He works for me, as it goes; bit of driving, bit of collecting, lays on a car or two. Anything else with you is strictly moonlight, I tell you."

Frank's face must have shown the surprise a hold-up victim's does because Elkin laughed for real. "I know, Frank – you always sent him to Sunday School, taught him how to blow his nose, an' now he's all tied-up with the naughty boys, with no end to what villainy he knows an' no end to what he'll do." With one of its unpredictable switches the face went back to being deadly serious. "I tell you, he's well tied-up, son – so if one goes down for a job, he goes down an' all, you know what I mean?"

But all Frank could do was shake his head, stunned. "You must have the wrong family; the wrong Butlers."

Elkin sipped at his drink, looked at Frank over the rim of the cut glass. "Oh, no, it's your Brian all right. The musical-box king?"

Frank slumped against the leather seatback, closed his eyes like someone in shock taking in the news of a close death. There was a long silence, marked by the click of the car's quartz clock. "So what do you want with me?" he asked at last. "Motors? Cheap motors?"

"Oh, we get those. You wanna go through your books."

Elkin explained it as if Frank were a child. "An' stolen motors –
you ask your boy."

Frank swore. "So, what is it? Money? More protection?"

For a few short seconds of fuse Elkin's nostrils dilated.
"Bins!" The word suddenly exploded on his lips. "Half a pair,
went missing on a job. Old Bill's got one half, your ol' man in
his poxy cab took the other..." His voice was growling in his
throat. "Bad luck, I s'pose, for him, wrong place wrong time,
went off with a vital piece of the evidence an' kept it as his
protection against anyone getting back at him..."

Frank managed to swallow. "He told you?" he asked.

"He left word. An' he left word where he hid 'em so's the
evidence could come up if anything happened..."

Frank swore in disbelief and twisted this way and that,
looked at Elkin, out of the window, back at Elkin again. It was
as if the movement could somehow help his mind to accept the
awful things it was being fed. "But ... he's ... dead ..." he
ended up saying.

Now Elkin rocked his own head sideways, like a teacher who
is just about keeping patience with a slow child. "So you can
see why I'm grievin' – and getting tired of waiting! Now – a
word in my ear tells me there's a strong chance your ol' man
left this word in a musical-box which has been shooting about
between your house an' your sister's like some yo-yo..."

At that Frank's head banged hard and despondently against
the car's side window. "I get it," he said. "Oh, mother, I get it
now ..."

"Well, I'm glad you do, Frank, son, 'cos now perhaps you'll
get it for me. Eh? Get it back off this *Paula*, is it?" Elkin sounded
straighter now, as if he were back to giving orders to one of his
men. "Just the tune, on a tape'll do. But I want it done
discreet, else it'll have to be a punishment job, an' I'd really
rather not, not with the Old Bills's interest in me an' your
family already..."

Frank stayed leaning against the window, his face a mask of

defeat, an outer numbness disguising God-knew what thoughts. But Elkin pushed him with an urgent edge on his voice. "Listen, he made a new roller, put a tune on it, a *clue* to where he hid my bins. Now, you get me that tune, Frank, an' I can get my bins, we can all relax, an' Frank Butler Motors won't get involved. 'Cos believe me, if I go down, you come with me. Like I said, you take a good look at your books. You're well in with us, your firm. . . "

Frank forced himself up off the window, shook his head. "I don't believe I'm hearing this. . . "

"Oh, you are, you are, my son," Elkin said, very quietly. Suddenly he flapped his paper again. "An' you know what? I think I've got that word, that netball one. Just come to me. 'Shooter'." He spelt it out. "Yeah, fits a treat. . . "

Frank was already on his way out of the car, though, a man who looked as if he might well be about to be sick in the Epping Forest undergrowth. But he wasn't. Somehow he held on to himself while he watched both Elkin's cars roar away without the offer of a lift back. And then he found a bench to sit on, put his head in his hands and he cried.

Mick Prescott twisted his cab into a faster-moving lane in the Commercial Road. With money still tight and the tourist season beginning he'd decided to see what he could pick up on a Saturday afternoon at the Tower. The Americans and the Japanese, he'd found, didn't mind taking the Tube to get out there, but they did like to throw themselves into a cab going back to their west London hotels. Deftly he weaved in and out like an ex-boxer should, went to driving one-handed when his cab radio crackled.

"Charlie four!" Terry came over faintly from the office in Plaistow.

"Charlie four."

"Mick – the 'Robin Hood', Epping Forest. Bloke wants a pick-up."

Mick pulled a face. "The 'Robin Hood'? You been at the wine gums? I'm up Aldgate!"

"Sounded a bit special, Mick. Definitely asked for you."

A solid jam had halted Mick: perhaps it helped him to make up his mind. "Got a name, has he?"

"Didn't give it. Sounded straight. You going or not?"

Mick looked up front at the nose-to-tail queue. "Yeah." He swung his cab out of it in a u-turn. "Tttt!" he chucked, for the benefit of no-one in the back.

At the 'Robin Hood' it was more the time for coming out than for going in, but the car park was still full enough for Mick to have to cruise up and down to find a place to park. Set where it was on the edge of the Forest the pub was a popular tourist attraction. But Mick frowned as he walked around his cab, took in all the transport. If the bloke wasn't here he'd never get a fare back. So it was with a mixed look of relief and surprise that he saw his brother-in-law Frank walking out from a line of cars.

"Mickey!"

"Frank! 'Ere, what's all this? I was up Aldgate..."

But Frank's red and watery eyes told a story of their own, even before the words. "Trouble, Micky. I'm in trouble, an' I need a bit of help ..."

Mick gave the distressed man a hug and led him towards one of the bars, where over an orange juice and a gin and tonic Frank cried some more and shared the whole of his burden. "I still can't take it in," he ended, "but if Elkin goes down, Micky, then so does my Brian – and my business with him." He looked round sadly at all the normal drinkers, like a man who's just been told he's got a serious disease. "Brian's had dodgy dealings – Elkin can tie me in like one of the gang ..."

Mick looked at his glass as if he wished he'd had the stronger drink. "It'll kill Ellie, that, and our Dolly won't never lift her head again ..."

Frank nodded greyly.

"So where is the old man's musical box?" Mick's eyes said he'd treat any answer a bit suspiciously on past form.

"Brian had it – but I never knew last night, Micky, I swear. Now your Paula's got it back, came and took it!"

Mick's eyes narrowed.

"But this is where you can help me, Micky. You got a tape recorder, a cassette thing?"

"Yeah, Deany must have three at least..."

"Right, well, I'll tell you what to do..." And with a loud blow of his nose Frank cleared his head and his tears and started to plan the rescue of his son and his firm.

You don't survive for long in Paula's part of the world if you can't pick up people's vibrations, can't hear the changes in a voice that come with nervousness or guilt, can't see the signs on someone's face of something going on. But then survival is also about disguising all that, so the balance in the end is a delicate one, and often comes down to intelligence or native wit. Like putting a couple of otherwise unremarkable facts together and making them fit like an I.Q. test. Which, in the end, was how Paula guessed her father knew more of what was going on than he'd admit.

First, there was walking in on him fiddling about with one of Dean's cassettes; fast re-winding something he'd just listened to, when the only time he'd ever been known to take any interest in anything like that was when he'd had a drink at a party and done his Tony Bennett. Then there was the open musical box on the sideboard – and her not getting the rucking she deserved for stealing it back. And his voice. *Too* light and normal, *too much* making of the jokes, when what he'd have really talked about after giving her a row was that second roller still fitted in the machine. And didn't his shirt pocket have something the shape of a cassette in it?

So, she asked herself, who had he recorded the roller for? *Capital Radio?* Who else was chasing the meaning of the tune?

Who'd got on to her dad to find out the answer? Brian himself? Uncle Frank? Could her Uncle Frank be in with Elkin as well? There were a lot of uncertainties. But Paula knew one thing. Her own mum and dad weren't any part of what was going on: if she didn't know that she didn't know anything: when she'd laid on the line for Nindy how innocent the Prescotts were she'd been telling the truth, she knew that for certain. Even if you don't want to admit it to yourself, you know when your parents are up to something – secret things like Christmas presents, the odd phone calls, someone at the door... So who was conning her dad? That was the question. Because someone was, that was for sure.

But Paula could only go round and round in circles with that till some other clue turned up: and meanwhile there was something better she could do, or at least do alongside – and that was solve the mystery of the message, and do it before anyone else did. *Then* she'd know what to do about it all, wouldn't she? Everything had to be clearer once she knew what her grandad had tried to tell her.

There was no thinking with Dean around and with her dad watching every move, so she said she was going to the library, and with a book under her arm for show she walked round the streets where she could think things through on her own, be a bit private. As she did, that Saturday afternoon, she passed normal houses, normal families, saw kids out to play – and, turning the corner by the swing park where kids screaming only meant having fun, she suddenly thought how crazy all this was. She should have been thinking about her swimming, or where she was going tonight, or *really* wondering what book to get out next, not trying to work out some clue which would threaten a big-time criminal. She stopped to stare at the kids playing, and she muttered a rude name at herself. What big words she'd used to her grandad when he'd had the chance to turn the glasses in, what brave stuff she'd spouted about standing up for justice! Because what a drag it was, carrying it all on your shoulders, being like some child queen who should've been playing games in the palace garden instead of deciding who had their heads cut off.

She turned her back and walked on. But the more she walked the more she knew the world just wasn't like that, whatever the picture books tried to tell you. Kids died of hunger in the big famines like everyone else, kids died in terrorist bombings, kids got kidnapped, kids got assaulted, kids got murdered with their parents when their family stepped out of line. You only had to look at the telly to know. It wasn't really so outlandish to be caught up in something like this. It wasn't even *unfair* when you looked at the unfairness of the world. It was just dead frightening, that was all.

As if her subconscious mind had decided that she should end up there, Paula found herself wandering in through the gates of the East London Cemetery, the place where she'd been so upset about leaving her grandad those weeks ago. She walked the path to the narrow grave where he was laid in rest down there with her grandmother, stopped and stared at the inscription on the headstone, the old part and the fresh, joined up with that patient word 'also':

NELLY MABEL BUTLER
1920 – 1979

*'Earth has one gentle soul the
less and heaven one angel more'.*

Also her loving husband

SAMUEL JAMES BUTLER
1918 – 1986

*'A loving, just and upright man,
steel true'. Re-united.*

She swallowed, tried to blink back a tear; decided to let it go. If you couldn't cry in a cemetery, where could you? And it did seem very comforting that he was so close to her, only feet away. If his spirit was anywhere it was definitely here. This was definitely his place, peaceful but within sound of the traffic he'd spent his life in, and the birds still chirping as if it was the country. "Grandad..." She said it out loud and it sounded right: not embarrassing when no-one was about, but natural. So, quietly, pretending to re-arrange some dried-petalled flowers, Paula knelt and spoke some more to him, the things she was bothered about. "Grandad ... what was you trying to tell me, eh? What am I gonna do about all this?" As if making some physical contact with him, her hand went to the necklace he'd made her, the silver name that had been one of the last things he'd created: and through the blur of her eyes she read his name on the stone over and over until it became nonsense: a series of characters about as meaningful as braille to the sighted. And with her mouth open from the crying she bent even lower. "I love you, Grandad." And then another thought. "You was ever so brave with Elkin." And she stared at the breeze ruffling the short grass, stalks cut too close to really bend, while in her head she pleaded with him in silence. "Help *me*, Grandad, eh?"

ten

"I can't make head or tail of that rubbish," Elkin told Brian as the tape Mick had made of the new cylinder came to the end. "You sure you put the poncin' thing in the right way round?"

"It only fits one way, Mr Elkin," Brian told him, turning to Leila for some flash of inspiration. But Leila could only shake her head. "'Less it's some other sort of music," she said, "Chinese, Indian, and I can't for the life see why it should be ..."

Words enough, though, to have Brian suddenly spinning the tape back to the beginning. "Funny you said that," he told her, "'cos that's the nearest I got." He played a few more seconds of the sound which definitely wasn't in the tonal scale or rhythm of anything familiar to them. "An' you know what, he knew about India, done his time as a boy soldier out there, so he'd know a bit about their music." But faced with a blank stare from Elkin he suddenly looked very unsure, like a kid in school who's put his hands up not knowing the answer but who's suddenly been asked. "Gotta be honest, can't think why he'd do it, though." His hand had flopped to his side.

But Leila could. All at once she was clicking her fingers and looking sharp at the stone-wall Elkin. "Could be, Charlie. They've got their whole *thing* all round here, the Asians. Pop songs, films – they're into everything." Elkin pulled a face which showed what he thought about all that. "Well, if the old man or the girl knew some of them, what a good place to hide this message. How many Pakis work for us?"

Elkin sneered. But it was the nearest anyone had got. And now Brian was jumping. "*She* has!" he said, "*she*'s got one! Paki cow helped her thieve it back!"

"So!" Leila looked from one to the other as if all seemed to sound more plausible. "Could be film music or anything. They're big on Indian films. Or say there's some traditional tune in, what? 'Passage to India' – then it could be in some passage they know."

Elkin thought about it: and suddenly like a striking snake he thrust his face at Brian. "Right, son! You do the collecting round the curry belt. Go an' ask some of your Indian mates what it is –"

With a laugh that didn't work Brian tried to tone the 'mates' bit down. "Yeah, O.K., Mr Elkin."

Now he was prodded by a short, strong finger, hard at the collar-bone. "An' don't you come back without an answer this time, you hear me? Could be said I'm running out of patience over all this . . ."

"Yes, Mr Elkin, will do." And fumbling up the cassette recorder from the desk Brian hurried out into the street.

In the real world, away from television plays, desk sizes don't count for a lot. Elkin sat at something cheap out of M.F.I., part of a humble cover in the bingo hall because his sordid rackets were really run by word of mouth and in his line of business you didn't put a lot on paper. Detective Inspector McNeill was another man whose office wouldn't impress, who worked in something more like a garage. But that meant nothing, either, because he was also one who preferred to keep the vital things very much in his head. And these days there was a steady trickle of very useful information coming into it, too. Brian had hardly left the *Empress* when the D.I.'s private line buzzed. McNeill threw his plastic spoon into his plastic curry, sucked his teeth and nodded at what one of his leg-men was reporting. "A'right sonny," he grunted, "stick wi' him. I got a guid feelin' we're gettin' somewhere here. . ." And from the look in his eyes something quite important was being filed in the system inside his head.

Meanwhile, a vitally important aspect of Narinder's life had been filed into another system. Her name, age and airport of destination were entered in the computer on the Air India stand-by disc; with a deposit paid on an economy ticket which could come up any time. Then, if Pratap could come up with the balance, she could be flown away to her new life within twenty-four hours. But Narinder didn't know this, and right now she was in the family living room, with her mother and Paula and the musical-box: not a social occasion, but on the same business all the others were about.

Kamal stroked the smooth, inlaid top of the heirloom. "This is beautiful, Paula. All these designs along the lid. You know, I've never heard one of these playing. We didn't have these in India."

"No? But you listen to this. This isn't the proper roller..." Paula looked at Narinder, sitting beside her sitar; and she played the cylinder while the eyes of both the girls were on the mother, hoping for some hint of recognition.

But Kamal only frowned, disappointed. "Oh, I thought it would be jolly, a dancy sort of thing. Is this something ... special...?"

Narinder looked apologetic. "The nearest we got was sitar, a raga, but I don't know enough yet." She plucked at a string on her own long, bulbous instrument. "See, we want to know exactly what it is. Thought you might..."

Her mother was quite emphatic, though, and shook her head at the foolishness. "Oh, no. I don't think so. It doesn't fit the form. You can ask your father, but I'm pretty sure it isn't raga."

If Kamal had been disappointed, the disappointment was much greater on the girls' faces. Narinder suddenly felt very flat and let down. If there was a slender hope she was clinging to it was Paula somehow putting her cousin down, getting something over on the people who were driving her away. All of which meant that if this music *was* a clue, then she and Paula had got to crack it first. "We'll ask him, then," she said. "Never know, do you?"

Paula shrugged. She didn't seem too hopeful, either.

Downstairs, Pratap was working by hand. The off-set litho was silent as he inked a hand roller and ran it over an etching, a piece of fine art work for a man who was labelling his own bottles of wine. Kamal came down the stairs with the girls, picked up some parcelling she'd been doing. "Have you got a minute to do a favour for these girls? They need the father's as well as the mother's opinion ..."

"Will you listen to something for us, Mr Sidhu?"

Pratap didn't take his eyes off the plate, which he was now inspecting through a magnifying glass, picking out a loose grain of metal with a fine pair of tweezers. "In a moment, please." He rolled on ink again, put a piece of glossy paper onto a pad of newsprint and pressed the block down firmly. As he peeled it off he seemed more satisfied this time.

"Dad, listen to this. Tell us if you've heard anything the same before ..." But Narinder guessed he hadn't. The real musician in their family was her mother.

Paula had been setting up the musical box on the far end of the bench.

She pulled the lever to wind the mechanism and released the catch quaintly marked 'going'. Once more the mysterious music played.

Pratap listened seriously at first, then he laughed, less polite than Kamal had been, and went back to his roller and plate. "Am I supposed to recognise that?" he asked. "What is it, a game, a joke, eh?"

"I've been telling Paula, it certainly isn't raga is it?" Kamal said.

The quiet man smiled at Paula. "I'll try very hard not to be insulted," he gave her a rare twinkle; and as if to cover the awkwardness, "Who's was this, did Nindy say? Your grand-mother's?"

"Yeah. Played it a lot. She was blind." Paula forced a laugh. "Not this roller though. Proper tunes." Her hand went to fingering the necklace at her throat. It was an awkward moment – ended suddenly by an impatient ring at the street door.

Ink on his fingers now, Pratap became alert. He went to the window and looked over the top of the black paint: he had changed, from the ordinary father they'd just glimpsed again to a very frightened man. "It's him! You know! The ink!" He waved at the floor, but no-one needed it explained.

Already, Narinder was pulling frantically at her friend. "Quick!" She took her to the stairs: but Paula resisted, shook her hold and grabbed instead for what they'd both left on the top. "He'll see it!" she hissed, and even as the door was unbolted she was grabbing the musical box into her arms and scuttling with it under the counter.

Kamal stared down at the two girls but somehow she kept her mouth shut: turned a hardened face towards the crook who was coming over towards her.

"Don' worry," he was saying, "don' get out your pram, I know you ain't due till next week; I ain't after money, as it happens." From out of his top he pulled the cassette recorder.

"We're a printer's," Kamal said, tartly. "We don't do mending of electrical goods."

But Brian was already into his patter: how he'd be prepared to let them off a month's insurance if they could name the tune for him. And Pratap, not yet in any position to go against this man, motioned with his fingers for him to switch his cassette on. Narinder, underneath, could only imagine her father stroking his beard nervously as he prepared to listen. But when the recorder played the same tune they'd played three minutes before on the musical box she almost hit her head on the counter. Staring wide-eyed at Paula she saw her just about manage not to drop the thing as both their mouths fell open with the shock. "But that's ..." her father was saying. For a terrible second Narinder thought he was going to give the game away; but he must have had a kick from Kamal.

"Know it, do you, squire? Well, thank God for that! I reckoned that myself – some pop song or a film from over your country."

But all Pratap could manage, with a catch in his voice, was, "Play it again, please. I'm needing to think..." The tape was re-wound and played again, while for the girls who were cramped beneath the counter the real pain was wondering what on earth Pratap could say at the end of it.

They were reckoning without Kamal, though. "Wait a minute, please," she said, coming to the rescue. "Yes! You remember it, Pratap. That beautiful film we saw on the video."

Narinder blew her cheeks out like an exhausted swimmer. What could her mother come up with? And there obviously wasn't going to be any help from her dad. His mind had been on the printing; faithful copying was his line, not inventing.

"Come on, then!" the man was saying.

But Kamal's words had over-lapped. "Oh, should I forget? Such a sad ending to it," she was going on, for all the world as if it were true. "You know, Pratap, that Calcutta film, with the little street thieves." Things suddenly went quiet as if she were still hoping for him to supply a title – and there was a really desperate edge to her voice as she looked out of the shop and finally found one – "Er, 'Across the Ro ...', 'Across the Market!' wasn't it? That's the one. 'Across the Market', I'm pretty sure."

Brian coughed. From underneath Narinder could feel the thump, thump, thump of the cassette being tapped upon the counter. "'*Across the Market*'?" He sounded very iffy about that.

"I'm right, aren't I? You remember it Pratap...?"

"Only very vaguely," Pratap put in, coming unfrozen.

A sudden fisted thump on the counter made everyone jump.

"I'll check, you know! I'll ask around. Only there's gotta be some words to it – what you said ain't enough on its own..."

"Oh, it's a couple of years old now," Kamal said. "I'll try to think – but you'll be finding people who remember..."

There was a very long pause: time for the girls beneath the counter to stare at one another and then have to look away because they couldn't stare any more.

"Oh, I do hope so, babe – for both of us, know what I mean?"

And to their great relief the next they heard was the scraping of boots and the slam of the street door. Even so, it took Narinder some seconds to decide to emerge, one cautious eye over the counter before helping Paula and the musical box up.

Pratap's beard was being rubbed more vigorously than ever. "So!" he said, angrily, thrusting his hands down to his sides. "What's going on here, please?"

And Kamal – exhausted with her valiant efforts – was very angry too. "What was that? What aren't you telling us? Why has that man got your grandfather's tune in his machine?"

Paula looked completely lost for words. "I can't tell you ... not for the minute," she said, asking with her eyes for them to please go easy on her. "I've gotta work it out, haven't I?" Her face lit up a little. "But I *knew* he'd got a tape... That mean's he's definitely after the same thing I am... "

"And what's that? I think you're owing us an explanation, Paula." Pratap, although he was turning to his roller again, had clearly been very shaken by what had happened. He was still looking at Paula every other blink.

In a pointless effort to distract, Narinder opened the musical box, stared at the cylinder, sighed, made to close the lid again. "See...?" she said, not knowing where she'd go from there, fingering the dull metal of the cylinder and giving herself a prick on the finger for her pains.

But nobody showed any sympathy. Paula stared at the

bobble of blood on the finger, then at Pratap's roller – and all at once her eyes had come alight with a sudden knowing.

"Excuse me," she said to Pratap, her voice very flat as if she were speaking in a trance, "could you lend me that screwdriver, please?" She was pointing at a yellow-handled electrical screwdriver held between clips on the wall behind him. Puzzled, Pratap took it down while Paula stared intently into her musical box. He handed it to her. Nobody said a word, everyone's eyes were too riveted on the girl and what she was doing: because awkwardly – she wasn't the craftsman her grandfather had been – she was unscrewing the cylinder from the mechanism, separating it from its bed at one end and its meshed-in cog at the other.

"It's not the wrong way round?"

But Paula only shook her head tightly, went on with the extrication, her tongue sticking out. "All right!" she said at last, when the heavy thing was free and balanced between her hands. "Now..." But to Narinder's surprise she didn't twist it over and attempt to set it back inside the musical box. Instead, with a quick apologetic look at Pratap she pulled a sheet of shiny paper onto the pad of newsprint, and carefully holding the cylinder at either end between thumb and forefinger, she rolled it over the paper, pricking little holes in it with the small, sharp spikes.

"It's not a tune at all," she said. She held the paper up to the light, turned it over, ran her fingers over the patterned lines of holes along its middle. "See?" Paula looked like the man who'd found the Dead Sea Scrolls. "You pricking your finger, talking about my blind nan, and your dad doin' his rolling. It all come to me, didn't it?"

And now Narinder knew. She knew what Paula was thinking, and she knew that she was right.

"Braille! That's it, isn't it?"

"Yeah, look!" The girl was so delighted her voice was shouting and Pratap had to put a finger to his lips. "See?

That's an 'R', that third shape, definitely. He taught me my name. 'R' comes in 'Prescott'!"

And suddenly Narinder felt something of the same sense of triumph, the slightest tremor of hope, a passing coldness halfway down her spine which came and then had gone – but which had registered. *Could* this mean there was something to have hope about? "Hey, Paula! Great!" She threw her arms around her friend and hugged her, a much tighter grip even than Tommy's.

"So is this braille message what that thug was after?" Pratap asked.

"Yeah, I reckon so. Better keep it safe, eh?" Paula folded the art paper and put it deep as it would go into her pocket. "And put this roller back, too." But her fingers had lost their calm now, and Pratap had to do it for her.

"But I still don't understand, Paula. Why would your grandfather want to give you a secret message?"

Paula looked at him, her mouth in the tight line the East End calls cagey. But suddenly Pratap wasn't going to have that. "Paula, you involved Narinder's mother and me in telling lies for you – to that man, who is certainly no friend to us. And he won't be forgetting it. So I do think you can tell us why you did such a thing." His long hands stroked the beard down his jawline, but his brown eyes looked very insistent and his voice had been firm.

Narinder kept quiet; she had tried to judge whether to cut in and save Paula again or not. But now she knew this had to come out. There wasn't any point in keeping anything back right now. She smiled at her friend, watched her finger her necklace again, and heard her quiet, flat voice start off at the night Sam had gone home shocked. She listened as Paula told them everything – about her scare on the ferry, about the house being turned over, about her grandad's need to have some hold over Elkin. And it was all nods and clucks and plain sailing until she got to the bit about the man who'd just been there, when suddenly she called him by his first name. 'Brian.' It sounded like some sort of swearing. Totally shocking.

"Him?" Pratap asked, pointing at the door. "*Brian?*" He stared at his wife, at Narinder, at Paula, flicked his hand and made a nervous cracking noise like a whip.

Painfully, Paula unrolled another piece of the truth. "He's my rotten cousin, isn't he?" she said. "That's how come he had a tape of the tune."

"Your cousin?!" Pratap looked at the girl, looked again at the door Brian had used. "Then why don't you tell your father? Why don't you let him deal with this cousin for you?" Pratap had gone so still he seemed almost to be in a state of shock. "If he's not a crook, too."

Paula, still confessing, let the accusation go. "No point telling him," she said, " 'cos he gave Brian the tape. He made it for him, I know that now."

Narinder turned her head from this new blow. So what was going on? Had she been conned by Paula after all? If Paula's dad was really in this...

"Someone's told him, that's all, an' he's scared like everyone else. It is *Elkin* we're talking about!" Paula was starting to defend her father. "He wants Elkin off our backs double-quick same as everyone else!"

So he can stay on ours, Narinder thought. But she didn't say it. It wasn't the right time – and, being fair, the truth of it wasn't quite as simple as that.

"Listen, my dad's not a crook and my mum's not a crook, I know that." Now Paula was beginning to cry as the Sidhus' understanding seemed to grow thin. "But I still don't know who I can trust out of all the rest."

Narinder watched Paula's real sobs catching in her throat; made worse, probably, by her needing to cry to stop all this. But beneath all the noise it made, Paula's and the sounds she and her mother made consoling the girl, Narinder heard an anxious voice murmur, "So, she doesn't know who she can trust... That's a club with a lot of members round here..."

which came from her father: and she saw the urgent stroking of his beard go on; which was definitely not a hopeful sign.

Sadly, Narinder was right to feel pessimistic. Pratap's immediate reaction to the news that someone as close as Paula had family members involved with the Elkin mob was to push firmly towards getting Narinder to India. That night, he must have instructed her mother, because on the Sunday she came to Narinder in her room and told her to get her suitcase ready.

Narinder's heart sank. The thin strand of hope she held through Paula finding the braille could be snatched from her in an instant by a sudden call to get in her father's car. But it wasn't until she tried to decide what she would take with her in that car, and what to leave behind, that the reality of the big change coming suddenly hit her. And however angrily she started on the job, however, she threw things to this side and that as if they didn't concern her, there was no other way it could end than just sitting there crying. All right, the saris and the salvar kameez were no problem: they got dumped on the pile for the suitcase. But what about the *Snoopy* tee-shirt? Or her bikini? And would she ever need her tights again? At last it all came sobbing out, all the frustrated, mixed-up emotion of being from an Asian family and born in London. It wasn't just a question of those two piles of clothes – one on one side for Asian occasions, one on the other for London times. Even in London – specially in London – talking your native cockney, wearing the latest gear, you could still be brought up short any time of the day by someone shouting 'Paki'; or by them just giving a long, hard stare, or keeping you waiting being served. While at the gurdwara, dressed in salvar kameez, kneeling on the sheet, someone near would tut at you if you lost the Punjabi words of a chant. Being what you were, you were a first, something new to the world, a different mixture, using British Telecom for chats with your mates but getting filthy messages stuffed through your letter-box by people who hated.

And it was hard, had been hard, would always be hard, and there were times when it got on top. But that was what your life was, and at least you were paced for it. And most important of all, Narinder knew, it was what you would choose again.

Now, with all that hard learning over, it was goodbye to it, pack up and get out. After all that survival stuff, after sorting her life out for herself, she wasn't going to have the chance to live it. Through her tears she stared down at a picture of Guru Gobind Singh – her favourite of all the gurus after Guru Nanak – the one with the most exciting stories, the one who gave them their names, *singh* and *kaur*, lion and princess, so that everyone would always know they were Sikhs. He'd had his battles to fight, he'd known what it was to be out on his own. But for him it had been different, she thought. He'd been going forward, making progress. She was going back.

A raised voice and the thump of feet suddenly straightened her up. Paula, shouting something polite to her parents, was knocking on the door and bursting in, all in one. "Nindy! Nindy!" She was well out of breath, throwing a plastic carrier onto the bed and collapsing after it. "I've had to bring it round here. The braille. My dad's got real suspicious, nearly had me, he'll cotton on, I know he will." Seeing nothing in the room, Paula pulled an old encyclopaedia out of the bag. "But I brought the book. Look, it's an old one of Grandad's – where he learned the braille himself, I reckon . . ." Still regaining her breath, she thumped the thick book onto the pile of salvar kameez.

"Well, don't leave it there," Narinder told her, "or it'll end up in Jullundur."

Only then did Paula look round, did she start to take anything in of the upheaval in the room. "Hey! What you doin', Nind?" she asked.

Narinder shook her head sadly, pointed to the suitcases which dominated the room for her. "Can't you see, girl?"

"No! Nind!" Paula looked about her as if she couldn't believe this reality.

137

"Yeah, sortin' out! An' not for no jumble sale, neither." And all at once Paula did seem to understand, did manage to see the tragedy from her friend's point of view. Her face showed its shocked sympathy, and despite herself it choked Narinder up. She waved at the pile flattened under Paula's encyclopaedia. "That's what's going with me —" and she nodded at the other, much bigger pile of clothes and belongings — "and that's what stays behind."

Paula shook her head, the deepest look of caring on her face that Narinder had ever seen. "I don't believe this is happening," she said in a voice which could hardly be heard.

"Well, it is!" Narinder suddenly sounded very matter-of-fact. "And them's the easy things. What about this?" She picked up a Walkman from the unsorted pile. "Eh? How long am I gonna go on hearin' our sort of stuff over there? How long 'fore this starts chokin' me up, thinking about you all. . .?" She waved her arm hopelessly, a sagging gesture which somehow encompassed Paula and the room and London. "What do you take out of your life?" she asked. "Eh? A picture of your mates, your school reports which say how good you're getting on?" She pointed to a folder of papers already on the rejected pile. "Soon start curling up, don't they? Not much use, miles from nowhere, with people you don't know, who do everything all different . . ." And the tears came again, but as much of anger now as of sadness. "You know what, Paula? The worst part is, it just ain't *hard*, choosing what to take from London — 'cos it's nothing! *Nothing*!" She whirled round in a sudden spin, kicked the huge pile of rejected things. "It ain't worth takin' any of this — 'cos I'm gonna have to change too much!" And with that big, dramatic gesture done she threw her arms round Paula's neck and sobbed out her heart: while Paula hugged her fiercely, her own tears coming now.

"Oh, Nind!"

Narinder felt helpless, hopeless. Wasn't there anything? Had it all got to end up without a fight? "Paula, you gotta help me . . ." Dribbling, sniffing, she looked at her pile of thin Asian clothing, still pinned down by the encyclopaedia, the book with the braille in, Paula's papers sticking out. She stared at it. Wasn't there any hope? With a brave jerk she broke away. "Paula, we gotta sort this – get rid of Brian and that Elkin . . ." But as suddenly as the fight had come it had gone again. She flapped her arm. Some hopes! Her chances all seemed so remote. "Perhaps I wouldn't have to go." But she couldn't put any conviction in it, even though she knew that this book and these papers were probably her only chance. "If we can't do that, girl, it's the end of everything!"

With an arm still round Narinder's shoulder, Paula backed her to the bed, sat her down with her, the book on their laps. Like someone cheering a depressed patient her voice sounded light and hopeful. "We'll do it, Nind, I tell you, we will! Look, I made a start. Got the first two words already. FIRE COMMITTEE."

"FIRE COMMITTEE?" Narinder's face was all doubt and lack of understanding. This was all so much pie-in-the-sky anyway.

"There's some more. Look, that's an 'R' next. It might make sense." Paula put her hand on her friend's, squeezed it. "Where there's life there's hope, eh?"

But Narinder's smile showed no real depth of belief in that. "Yeah," she said. "So they reckon. . ."

eleven

Paula bumped her way along Green Street, all hard stares and curses for not looking where she was going. But she didn't notice – didn't even care that she was out after school time and still in her uniform. Go on a message to Uncle Frank's showroom or fly to the moon – with what she'd got on her mind, her clothes and where she was going didn't seem to make any odds. Not even the thought of seeing her uncle for the first time after her raid on his house could make her feel any worse. It was all too heavy, this business that had settled on her back since that sad turn-out in Nindy's bedroom.

"Mind out, can't you!"

Poor old Nindy! It was getting really close, must be, with her dad making her actually put things in her case. And a real shock, walking in on her doing it. Another time she'd walk in and find out she'd gone for good, no time for goodbyes or nothing! It was terrible! Paula just about stopped at a kerb. And not only terrible for Nind, either. It was going to be rough for her, too, her best friend going, like losing an arm or a leg, or some really close person like Grandad. Sighing, Paula felt in her pocket, ran her fingers over that spoon Nindy had made and given her to give to Grandad: just something to touch, like her *Paula* necklace, something never to be without.

"Watch your elbow, then!"

"Sorry!" And what about Grandad? What about his braille mystery, those words he'd pricked out with the musical box roller? They didn't make sense and they should have: FIRE COMMITTEE ROOM ELLIOTT STREET. She'd thought she'd have an easy answer when that was worked out instead of more stuff to play on her mind. What had he been thinking? Did

Elliott Street ring a bell? Or was it jumbled, some message all mixed up which didn't mean what it looked like, like in a crossword? Well, they'd tried, she'd tried. Hadn't she gone barmy trying to work it out? But there were always too many letters over for it to be like that.

"That's a baby there!"

"Sugar!" Paula disentangled herself from the reins wrapped round her legs, hopped out of the noose, looked up, and was surprised to find herself where she needed to be: outside *Frank Butler Motors*, Uncle Frank's car showroom: all closed up now but just as she expected, her uncle moving about inside. She rang the bell beside the glass door.

"Come in, love, come in." The door was opened quickly, smiles through the glass then a hug and a kiss on the cheek: just right, never too much, never soppy, Uncle Frank, always straight: didn't deserve a son like Brian in a hundred million years, Paula thought.

She fished the *Motor Traders' Retail Price Guide* out of her pocket, gave it to him. "Mum said sorry, she didn't know how she came to take this home."

Uncle Frank weighed it in his hand, tapped it like a preacher with a Bible. "Oh, these things happen: but I can't do a proper deal without this. Thanks for bringing it round."

"'S'all right." Paula stepped back towards the door, wanted to get away. What she'd got on her mind had to be sorted out – and besides, who knew whether rotten Brian might be lurking about.

"Oh, don't go, love. You can come in for a minute, now you're here, can't you? Give your old uncle two minutes? You seen my office since I had it done up?"

Paula looked at the man. He seemed tired and sad, but putting on a bit of sparkle the way people do – the sort of cover up which is somehow meant to tell you that's what it is – a sympathy thing, really. Poor old Uncle Frank ... With a smile Paula followed him into his office, tried to show a bit of interest.

And he was right, he had had it done up. Instead of the painted wallpaper it was all lined with wood: dark and shiny, but too much like the take-aways for Paula.

"It's ever so nice . . ." she said. But her voice tailed away as she suddenly saw her uncle's desk: and not the material or the style of it, but what was on it: all white doylies spread out with pastries on them, and champagne glasses, and an ice-bucket with a frosty bottle of grape-juice leaning in it. "Here, is this a car place or a caff?"

Uncle Frank threw his head back and forced out a laugh, like a sea-bird on the catch. "A caff? The very best non-alcoholic grapejuice, the finest pastries in Shepherd's Gate, and you call it a *caff*?"

Awkwardly, Paula joined in the laugh. "Yeah, well, you know what I mean – you got someone coming, then?"

"No, not coming. Come. You're here, aren't you?" Her uncle said it with meaning and a sort of old-fashioned flourish – the way he gave out his Christmas presents. "Sit yourself down, love, make yourself at home."

Gingerly, Paula sat on a chair. This was something new, this was, and a bit uncomfortable she felt. Somehow it didn't have the ring of being right, here on her own behind the scenes. She counted the wine glasses. There were three of them . . . "What is this?" she asked.

Uncle Frank was being busy and professional with the ice bucket. "Well, love, it's not a birthday, it's not Christmas, and it's not an anniversary. It isn't even the Chinese New Year." The mushroom cork went pop. "It's a make-up party."

"Make-up?" Paula's hand went to her cheek. She'd heard of Tupperware and nightie parties, but not –

"Not cosmetic make-up. It's a party for me . . . to make-up with you!"

Paula pulled a face, but felt it going red: just then she could have done with some cosmetic make-up, as it went. . .

"Listen, love, we've always been the best of friends, haven't we?" Uncle Frank poured the grape-juice, a champagne-looking drink with golden bubbles. "Think of those holidays we used to have, and Christmas-time – I've always thought we got on like a house on fire, you and me..."

"Yeah, me an' all, but why've you got to...?" Paula waved her glass at the table, couldn't put into words what she wanted to say. And anyway, wasn't that business back at his house best not talked about any more? But she knew that Uncle Frank had never been one to dodge an issue. When he came to their house and he was too hot, or he needed a drink, he said so. Now she watched him take a sip from his own glass, put it down, come to the point. "We need to make up because my Brian risked spoiling our friendship, Paula, by doing something unforgivable; playing that trick to get into your house and taking Nan's and Grandad's musical box away. I feel guilty over that, Paula, I feel bad because Brian's my son."

It was still hard to know what to say. A lot of things were definitely best left not talked about, Paula reckoned. You only had to show people how you felt, you didn't have to announce it all the time. "Oh, Uncle..." she managed. But she did love him: he was a good old stick, putting this on to make things right.

"I know ... Now, I can really recommend these, fresh cream." Perhaps sensing her embarrassment he slid her a doyly of pastries.

"Ta."

"Also, I wanted you to know that our kitchen floor cleaned up O.K. Auntie Ellie thought you might be worried about that."

"Oh, yeah, good." Quickly, Paula bit into an exploding eclair. That subject was definitely best left alone.

"So you've got your musical box back all right, and we're still the best of friends, yes?"

"Yes!" Paula looked up at him, smiled.

"Then we'll drink to that, eh?" He raised his glass, looked

for a moment as if he were at a dinner and dance. "To the family. May it never be spoiled or divided." He drank, his eyes staring at her down the flute of the champagne glass.

"Cheers." Paula drank too. "The family."

He refilled their glasses and forced another fancy on her. "But there was something else," he said. "I wanted to explain about that musical box, Paula. Because I think you're old enough to understand why Brian took it from you for a day or so."

Paula looked up sharply from her skirmish with the cream. All at once he looked like the motor trader getting down to business. And his voice had changed; he was speaking higher, with that funny roof-of-the-mouth sound people make when they're saying something for the record.

"It's not a reason I'm over the moon about, mind, but if you don't know it already, love, then I'm afraid it's down to me to tell you today ..." He was staring at her, as if he were waiting for her face to show him what she knew: but the cream was a good cover-up, gave her plenty to do with her expression as she twisted her mouth this way and that beneath her tissue.

"Yeah?" she gave him a big, innocent stare.

"Well, perhaps it's not down to me to tell. Down to someone a bit special, perhaps ..." He coughed and waved his cigarette at the table. "You'll have noticed there's three wine glasses ..."

Yes, she had, at first, but she'd forgotten. So, who's was the third one? She stared at his face for an answer. "Your Brian? Auntie Ellie coming, is she?"

"No, it's Mr Elkin. And he's here."

Paula spun round. Because the voice hadn't come from Uncle Frank. It had come from behind her. Quiet, kind, menacing, and right behind her chair. All at once her back had turned to ice, her heart seemed to have stopped, petrified. Elkin! The big man! In here! And him looking at her right now through a pair of fine, gold glasses! She stared, disbeliev-

144

ing, as Elkin sat down, took the glass Frank had handed him, and smiled at her.

"See this face, Paula!" he said in a soft voice. "It's heavily made up, got to be, because underneath I'm green with envy." He leaned forward, gently touched one of her hands with both his own. "I'm envious of your family, Paula, all so close – an' isn't it appropriate that this little word I'm having with you should be in here, sweetheart? *Frank Butler Motors* – so much a part of what your family's about. Eh, Uncle Frank?"

Paula darted a look across at her uncle who was nodding, tight-lipped, begging with his eyes for her to see things the way Elkin was putting them.

"Your dear old Uncle Frank, running a nice business, your lovely mum working here to help him, well paid, helping keep ends up at home ... Yes ..." He looked around him – "This place is a very important part of your life, don't you reckon? As a family?"

Paula had to nod. When he put it like that it was true.

His hands left hers, went up to her cheeks where they held her, very gently: surprisingly smooth, with a faint perfume about them. "So why destroy it, sweetheart? Why jeopardise it? Why let Bri be a scapegoat?" His voice was low and hypnotic, his hands there cupping her cheeks, and she felt light in the head, couldn't believe that this was Elkin and all this was happening. "If Bri goes down for something naughty he did, if I go with him – an' you know what I mean, don't you? – then all of this goes with him. Swoosh! Down the pan." His hands described the downward movement, touched her neck and her shoulders, then away to make a flying pattern in the air. "At the very least your Uncle Frank goes out of business, your mum loses a good job, and no Butlers or Prescotts hold their heads up for years to come. And for what?" His hands came back to the table where he poured himself another glass of grape-juice.

Paula swallowed, tried desperately hard to focus on the face, to see Elkin not as a man with a very soft touch but as a villain, the man who Grandad had told her ran their part of the East End, the one who'd had their house turned over. But it wasn't easy, not with someone as persuasive as this.

"And for what, eh? Everything goes down the shoot for the sake of turning me in?" He laughed, tucked his chin into his neck, tapped with his fingers on his chest to show what a minor catch he'd be. "Old me? But then again, what's the price of keeping all this? Just turning over to me half a pair of glasses that got dropped in the wrong place, fell out in your grandad's cab." Smiling, stroking her with his voice, Charlie Elkin made it all sound very reasonable, like a helpful maths teacher taking you through a difficult equation. "Because he didn't really want them given in, did he? He never gave them in himself. He hid them, for some reason of his own. An' he's gone now, darling, rest his soul, and they're no earthly use to anyone but me, now, are they?"

It was a good job he'd mentioned her grandad then because it suddenly pulled Paula back from the persuasive web his words had been spinning. "I ... I don't know nothing about this, honest," she said. Whatever was right to do, she couldn't afford to let Elkin know she knew anything.

The big, smooth man sat down and took a fork to a fancy, began eating it the way you're supposed to, gave the impression by the way he sipped at his drink that the party was the important thing, the being together. "Don't blame Uncle Frank now, will you? I asked him to arrange a meet."

Paula smiled and shook her head, for some reason tried to look as nicely back at him as he had been looking at her. And it was then while she was smiling that he got in under her guard, held her eyes with his while he said what he wanted, took advantage of her exposed face to make it flush. "I think you *do* know something about this business, Paula. It might be through that musical box or it might be some other message you've had got to you." His eyes held her so that she couldn't look away. "But I don't want to involve you in anything dodgy, my love ..." He seemed to see right into her, almost as if the message she'd been trying to decipher was written somewhere in her mind and he was reading it. "But I do want you to know the score, so's if you do come across them bins, or you know anything to lead people to them, like I think, then you're gonna tell your uncle here." He swallowed. She swallowed. "Because remember, all his living, all this, Paula – and his family name – your family, an' all – is gonna hang on that. All right?"

All Paula could do was nod, and swallow again, and reach shakily for her champagne glass: while Elkin sat back, waved a hand at Uncle Frank. "What a nice kid!" he said, beaming. "A really nice kid. And don't believe all you hear about Charlie Elkin, sweetheart." He tapped his chest. "I can be a really generous sort of uncle an' all, you know – which I shall look forward to proving to you one day, eh?"

To avoid his gaze Paula looked at the remains of her pastry on the plate. "Yeah..." she said. But even as she stared his fork came into her vision to spike the pastry, and hypnotised she followed it to his smiling face as he opened his mouth and fed it in.

"Just so long as you remember which side your cream's on, eh, love?" he murmured.

Narinder had read somewhere that every person someone meets, every encounter they have, changes them a bit. No-one is ever quite the same person at the end of a day as they were at the end of the day before. And that certainly seemed to be true for Paula Prescott. When they'd said goodbye in her bedroom, had worked out that braille message amongst all the jumble of clothes, it had seemed like nothing would stand in the way of them finding the evidence Paula's grandad had hidden away, and nothing would stop them getting it to the police. But today, in school, Paula had suddenly gone all distant, just pulled a face when she'd said she couldn't work the clue out, even changed the subject and gone on about forgetting her P.E kit. So what had happened to Paula to change her from the day before? Who had she met? Or had she pricked her own finger on the musical box and suddenly decided that blood was thicker than water'?

With her head in her hands Narinder watched her friend through her fingers, sitting there pretending to take an interest in the first lesson, smiling at the French *assistante*, making out she was enjoying the crummy jokes about Monsieur Duval and his *voiture*. Usually she was banging her head on the desk, here at the back, the jokes were so painful. But today she was nearly choking herself, laughing. At the end of forty minutes, though there was a chance to sort things out: so Narinder took it, in the cloakroom. Not a confrontation, nothing in the open, but just a bit of putting on the pressure. When they were on their own, over by the sinks, she pulled out her copy of the message and waved it again at Paula, looked hard into her friend's eyes for some hint of what was going on.

"Haven't you got any idea what this means?" she asked. "'FIRE COMMITTEE ROOM ELLIOTT STREET'?"

Paula screwed up a paper towel and threw it at the bin, missing. "Only what I said." She sighed. "I dunno, Nind."

It was a big sigh, seemed to be about a lot more than deciphering the clue. So Narinder tried to whip up some of yesterday's enthusiasm, just to see what effect it had. Because all at once it seemed like it was that or have it out with her, call her a traitor again, and she wasn't ready for that big step, not yet.

"Tell you what, then – if it isn't all jumbled up – let's read it straight. Let's find Elliott Street, go down there an' see. I don't half sound familiar, Paula..."

"Yeah, if you like – no harm..." But Paula's answer still lacked any bite, and suddenly Narinder had to go further. She put her hands on Paula's shoulders and turned her square. "Paula – I just keep thinking of my dad's face when we tell him we could get your stinking Brian put away..."

Paula's face seemed to force a smile from somewhere. "Yeah, Nind. Too right. . ."

"We'll have a look after school, then, eh? There's a map up the library. We'll get down there straight away, 'fore my dad misses me. Eh?"

"Yeah. O.K."

"*Today*." She knew there'd be no time the next day, not with a school trip to the Thames Barrier laid on: Paula could have all sorts of excuses for hurrying home after that sort of late finish. And Narinder saw her suitcase standing there at the top of the workshop stairs. Who knew whether tomorrow wouldn't be too late anyway: whether by this time she mightn't be thirty thousand feet over Greece, or somewhere? It was an answer she needed, and quick. "A bit of action, eh, Paula? A bit of – what do the police say – a bit of footwork?"

"Leg-work!" Paula had to smile, and she patted Narinder's face. "Footwork's what you done with Tommy at the dance."

With the faintest feeling of having got somewhere, Narinder smiled herself, and let herself be led back into the corridor. You never knew, she thought, she could have been wrong. She could have been too sharp and just imagined Paula Prescott's cooling off.

But then no-one seemed able to feel sure about Paula. In Elkin's office behind the bingo there was the strong feeling in the air that things were hotting up – but which way the Prescott girl would jump in the heat was something no-one could sound certain about.

"I definitely got home to her." Elkin was sitting behind his desk, smart in a blazer. "You could see it all over her face. But we've gotta make sure, right?" It wasn't often Elkin explained himself like this to the others, and they, the experienced Barrett, the violent Ron Martin and the chameleon Leila Duke were all looking nervous. One wrong word and there could be an explosion.

"It makes a lot of sense," Leila put in. "We just double-up on everything..."

"Right!" Elkin got up. He stubbed a finger at Barrett and Martin. "So you two take Frank Butler an' his idiot son, one each – and Lei, you take the girl. I wanna know what all of 'em are up to, every last twitch, you got it?"

"Yeah." Martin had a hand on the door already. Definitely a survivor, was Ron.

But Leila held back, seemed to want some sort of clarification. And like a cornered tiger Elkin snarled. "What you waiting for? She comes out of school soon, don't she?"

So Leila clamped her mouth firmly shut. She just looked at the king of the East End, who'd suddenly got the jitters over some kid he should have topped. But it was as if he knew what she was thinking.

"I can't take a chance!" he said. "I dunno what arrangements that stupid old bastard made!"

In days gone by Elliott Street had seen horses and carts, children in bare feet, incendiary bombs, pig-bins, street parties and both National Front and Young Socialist marches. In two long terraces of three-ups three-downs, it had been built at the turn of the century for skilled workers in the docks, for office clerks – and the occasional family who could run to a Ford. Now it was a street which seemed to be inhabited by cars. Being terraced, there were no garages, and the first impression of the road was of metal: only by walking the pavement did a sense of people come. And then it was the colour and the contrasts which struck: some gaudy houses, some drab; some doors portico'd, some unshaded and peeling; some shut tight against dust and neighbours, some spilling out with children playing on the pavement in a whole world of languages. And the bare feet, when they skipped, were bare mainly from choice these days.

Even before she turned the final corner Narinder knew what

this place was. The name had definitely rung a bell, and now she knew what it was: her family just never talked about it in terms of the street name, that was all.

"I knew I knew it!" she told Paula. "Our temple's down this street, our gurdwara."

And from the corner they could see it, a large building in the same brick as the houses, with the same slate roof: except across the front on a large wooden board there was a fancy piece of sign-writing in English: SIKH TEMPLE.

Paula shook her head. "I don't get it, Nind, It's the only big place. 'FIRE COMMITTEE ROOM ELLIOTT STREET' – I thought there'd be some office or something..." But there wasn't. They walked down one side of the street and up the other, looking hard at every house, every door sign. And when they came back to it, they were still left with only the gurdwara as being anything other than an ordinary house.

"Paula, I'm telling you! It's got to be this," Narinder said.

But Paula, on edge, replied as if she were talking to an idiot. "So what does it mean, then? Committee Room? They don't call a temple nothing like that, do they?" Her hands and her face said she knew darned well they didn't.

"No, it's a gurdwara in Punjabi, that's all. *The guru's door.* It's not known as anything else, only temple..."

"Well, then..." Paula backed a pace and stood looking up at the large, square building as if somehow a clue might come sliding off the roof like a loose slate. "Funny, though, even calling it a temple. Hasn't got no domes and things, has it? All ordinary, really."

"Well, it wasn't built for it." Narinder was getting impatient. Surely Paula knew there'd been no Sikhs here when this street was built. "We use what's here, that's all. This must've been something else before..." And with those words the slate slid. And almost like dodging the imaginary drop, Narinder jumped. "Here, Paula, what would it have been in your grandad's day, this place?" she asked. "Because people like

151

him don't always see things change, do they? Go out of their way sometimes to talk about places by their old names..."

"Yeah?" Paula didn't sound so excited about that. But at that moment a door opened across the road and out came an elderly woman with a shopping bag: just the sort who might have lived in Elliott Street for years, seen all the changes going on.

Even before the door had slammed Narinder was over to her. "'Scuse me," she said. "We're doin' a project for school, and we was wondering what that temple was over there, like years ago. Wasn't always a temple, was it?"

The old lady looked at her, seemed to know all about school projects because she didn't question her wanting to know. And her eyes seemed to mist as she looked at the evening sun giving the faintest tinge of gold to the large roof. "Lord, no," she said. "The Working Men's Club, that was. Elliott Street Working Men's Club."

Narinder turned round to face Paula across the street. "The Working Men's Club," she called.

"Yes, and lovely it was, I can tell you, before all your television." The old woman had got into her stride, almost as if Narinder might be recording her for posterity. "A bit of entertainment, Saturdays; nice gardens of a Sunday; a bar, billiards for the men ..." Her face suddenly clouded. "All changed now, though." And the way she looked it was almost as if she were blaming Narinder for it.

"Yeah. Ta. Well, thanks ever so much."

Narinder began to go; but the old woman wasn't finished; raised her voice to be sure the girl had it all straight. "You ask the old people round here. Lovely, it was, when there was such things as working men to use it. Elliott Street Working Men's Club." She called it like a sort of forgotten chant.

Narinder crossed again, still frowning. So had they got any nearer? It took only a quick look at Paula, though, to know for certain that they had. She was clenching her fists and doubling up like a skier in some silent dance of triumph.

"That's it!" Paula hissed. "It rang a bell with me an' all, Elliott Street, only I never said... It's Grandad's club. This used to be the club he went on about sometimes! 'Strewth, Nind, it's a good job I got here 'fore Brian or Uncle Frank. They'd know it straight off!"

Narinder looked hard at her friend. By her excitement was she helping now, then? Back on the track? Was she definitely ready to find the committee room inside this place and do for her cousin Brian? Well, it looked like it. But she still couldn't be really sure. *Your best friend's always a river away*, her mother said. And wasn't blood thicker than any water? No, Narinder decided, she definitely still couldn't be sure.

And at that moment she'd have been even less sure of her chance of getting out of the flight to Jullundur if she'd noticed what was going on further along the street: a young woman in a mac stopping the old age pensioner who'd helped them, getting into conversation with her: a young woman who was Leila at her sweetest, talking to the old girl about the kids over the road, and the good old days...

When Narinder mentioned Paula's name at home it seemed as if it had all rebounded on her anyway.

"You were late coming home tonight, Narinder." For some reason the meal had been ready early, and now her father was sitting there doing his head-of-the-table thing, while her mother stayed out of it and just kept the chapatis coming.

"I was with Paula." Narinder dipped into the yoghurt, balancing the chapati on her long fingers.

"Paula? She is dangerous!" Pratap threw down his food and shook a finger at her. "With all this criminal business around her, you should be staying well clear." He wiped his mouth on a tissue, had forgotten his meal now. "All these secret messages in braille, a criminal family... We want none of that, do you hear me?"

But he had raised his voice, and that suddenly angered

Narinder. He'd raise his voice to her all right, but not to the real criminals. He'd run away from them! She coughed, choked on that last mouthful. "Oh, yeah?" she heard herself shouting back. "She's only trying to help us!" And she shouted it so loud she knew she had to believe it.

Now her father's voice was low again, quiet and suspicious. "What are you meaning, *help us*? How can she help us? What has she said to you, this girl?"

Narinder swallowed on her anger. "Not a lot. Not ... straight. But she would help us if she could, I know she would."

Two more chapatis floated onto the table, and Kamal spoke, quietly, thoughtfully, taking the heat from between father and daughter. "She is a friend, Nindy. With family problems. She has her own river to cross, I'm thinking..."

"I don't know about all that." Narinder leant forward, tried appealing to their common sense. "Listen, Dad – just say that Brian and Elkin and all that gang did get caught and all got put inside ..." She stared at his face, at the eyes she'd known for ever. "... If they did all get put away, Mum and me wouldn't have to go to Jullundur then, would we..."

She watched him, saw the hands come up to stroke the beard downwards as she knew they would.

"Oh, that's a very big thing to say, Narinder..."

It was; she'd never asked a more important question to that face in her life. "Yeah, but..." And she had to have an answer. Love it or hate it till she died, she had to have an answer from him.

But it was her mother who spoke; calmly again, and as surprising as only she could be. "But if it were said, Pratap? If this trouble became all sorted out, would we still have to go and share that small house with your parents in the Punjab?"

Narinder closed her eyes. She hadn't expected a question so weighted from her mother: she hadn't known that she'd get this support. And hardly daring to listen she heard her quietly going on. "There will always be trouble here in England – racial, colour prejudice – that will never go right away, no-one can pretend it will: no more than the Hindus will stop hating the extremist Sikhs in the Punjab. But if this *extra* horrible business got stopped...? What about then, Pratap?"

Pratap had got to the bottom of his beard, was irritating it with his fingers now. "You're not saying this little girl Paula can do that, are you?"

"No. Not necessarily." Narinder tried to sound so very reasonable, tried to make it sound like a school debate. "But if it got stopped *somehow*...?"

Her father's hands came from his face, opened up as if he were receiving a large gift. "Then yes, we could stay, I suppose, I could build this up again." He shook his head, though, his big, dark, sad eyes again the dominant feature. "But what a big *if*, princess..."

Narinder stared at her plate, watched the bright patterns on it go swimmy; heard the swish of her mother's clothing as she went to put her arms round her husband. "A big *if*," the woman said quietly – "but I am thinking *hope* is a bigger word ..." And all at once there was no way that Narinder could look either of them in the eye.

twelve

There was something the same about Mr Elkin and Detective Inspector McNeill. So Paula thought later. And it was in the hands, the way they both tried to hypnotise you with them, using them to help say what they wanted – like an actor or a conjurer or a politician – and then the way they both touched you with them like some pope. And what that told you, underneath it all, was that they both wanted to underline all their words with action. But at first that evening, when she walked in to find McNeill there and waiting for her, she felt too scared to think anything at all. Not that she was asked to *say* a word, thank God. Just listen, and feel the life in the hands, that's what she had to do.

She pretended not to know the policeman at first; or, at least, to be very slow to remember. He was standing with his back to the big window, and she had to squint to see him; and even his position wasn't accidental, she realised after. It was all to do with being on top.

"Oh, I'm sure you remember me, lassie," he said to her frown, giving a little look of surprise for her mum and dad. "We had a wee meeting in the passage, when your grandfather was caught up in that ... unpleasantness." He took his hand out of his pocket for a measured wave at the room.

Paula nodded. "Oh, yeah, I remember now."

"Only, I'm just passing by," the man said, "chasing up loose ends, you might say." Now his hand was in his thick hair, scratching it as if he were truly puzzled. "And I do seem to have seen you around an awfu' lot – being a bit active, you might say, young Paula. Looking at temples, taking tea with strange company ..." And his hand lighted gently on her shoulder, gave it a squeeze. "Just youthful energy, you'll say. Living life to the full? Well, that's fine." He folded his arms across his chest, something like a wrestler in a photograph. "Only when we get a mite too energetic our games sometimes get too boisterous, eh? We get a wee bit excited, and then it's tears before bed!"

Paula said nothing: she couldn't: but he'd been watching her face the way Elkin had – and she knew her expression must have told its own story.

"You got the place all straightened up, then, Mrs Prescott?" He changed his tack, went for her mum now.

But Dolly kept her answer straight, sounded sarcastic more than guilty. "Oh, you did know, then," she said – as if therefore the police should have done something about it.

"Aye – we knew. An' it's a weird thing, that," McNeill went on, his voice getting louder as he made his points – "it's a weird thing how people's first reaction isnae 'murder-polis!' but 'keep it quiet, keep it under y' hat'. An' I never can figure out why. People think the villains o' this world hold all the aces ..." And here he stretched his palm, like a boy for the strap – "But you show me a wee handful o' guts, a small enough dose of courage to sit on a kiddie's hand, an' I can do the rest." And his hand went to his heart, meaning it. "That's a solemn promise, mae friends."

He went then. Just that final touch of Paula's face, a finger on the forehead. "But remember, wee lassie, when it comes to ears, mine's the one for talking intae. An' I'm very, very discreet."

The door had hardly closed behind him, though, before her dad was hissing at her, "I wanna word with you upstairs, on the quiet."

And it didn't take long before he got up to her, coming in quietly and closing the door. Mick was never a man to use side streets when the main road was clear. He came straight to the point. "Uncle Frank's told me. You had tea with Charlie

157

Elkin! Paula, girl, that scares me!" He stood in the middle of the bedroom, thumping a finger into his chest. "You know that?"

"I didn't ask to. It was Uncle Frank..."

Mick looked at the ceiling, suddenly crouched down at her level, sitting on the bed. "Paula," he said in a dead, flat voice – "you know where them glasses are, don't you?"

Paula snorted: a stupid sound but it was all she could do. "No! Blimey, Dad, you gone silly?"

"No, I ain't!" he snapped. He was the boxer, the fighter, anything but silly, and knowing all about tight corners. And, wily, because just as suddenly he softened again, sat down next to her on her bed and nervously smoothed the duvet. "Paula, love, this is our family hanging in the balance, you know that ..." He was staring at her, the blue eyes she knew better when they laughed. "Don't that come first, eh? If McNeill gets hold of them glasses, right or wrong, we're finished, love, believe me." He looked round the room as if somewhere he'd find the words to convince her. "What about dear old Uncle Frank, always put you first, he has, been a good old stick to you. He'll go right down the drain, girl, take my word, guilty-by-association if McNeill gets hold of those bins." His bright, fighter's eyes suddenly began to fill. "And your mum, she won't be able to face a neighbour for years when all that lot comes out: think of it, a trial, your cousin Brian, perhaps your Uncle Frank in the dock, the name of Butler all over the papers next to Elkin." He was really very close to crying, and so was Paula. "*Listen* to me, love."

Paula was. She'd taken in every word, the way she had with the others. But this was no Elkin speech, no McNeill spiel. This was her dad, and he was talking from his heart: didn't even need to use his hands. "I know it don't seem right to decent people, letting a little toe-rag off the hook – or letting a big villain off for that matter: but it's got to be done, love, if we can do it. For our family. For us. You understand?"

Paula did, like *anything* she did, and she nodded. There was nothing worse in the world for a kid like her than seeing someone she loved so all cut up.

"So, do you, love? Do you know anything?"

Of course she did. And a word now to her dad and all this torment would be over. Blood *was* thicker than water. No-one could blame anyone for sticking up for their family. She put her hand to her mouth, as if to help keep her voice down. All at once it was just the two of them, her and her dad.

"There you are!" But it was Dolly as well now, gathering coloureds for her washing machine load. "Anything rather'n dry up, Micky Prescott!"

"Gawd, that'll be the day." But the moment had passed and Mick had to go. And Paula made sure she put her light out quickly, in case he was tempted to come back. She knew she was going to toss and turn without a wink of sleep all night: but now she knew this problem was something she'd got to go through and get sorted – without anyone, not even her dad, telling her how she was supposed to think.

Ms Rogers had been building up to the Thames Barrier trip for ages. It was the end of a long project they'd been doing in Social Studies about man's achievements – a subject on which Tommy Parsons kept boasting he'd got a juicy secret file of his own – but it wasn't till she got there that Narinder began to realise what the teacher's enthusiasm was all about.

The coach set them down outside the exhibition centre, a square, plastic-looking building: and with the cynical shouts which passed for humour they went inside for a pretty boring time. With Paula quiet again, the others pushing and jostling, Narinder found herself in a small modern foyer, all perspex, videos, working models and dummy pipework. "The eighth wonder of the world," Ms Rogers enthused, as the model Barrier hydraulically rose into place.

159

"Clever old design," said Scott. "You could do one in metalwork, Prescott, when you've got the 'ang of spoons!"

But the class was quieter already; and when they went into the small theatre for the audio-visual show they seemed ready to be impressed. Standing leaning on the barriers, football-style, facing the screen, struck by lightning, stormed upon, flooded, swamped in sight and sound, even 3R stayed a bit quiet. And it was a good job that everyone was facing front engrossed in the presentation, because Narinder Kaur Sidhu at the back was quietly crying. The story of the growth of London and the parts played by successions of newcomers from the Roman invaders to the modern immigrant workforce – navvies, artists, engineers – seemed almost to have been written to underline the way she felt about things, and to make it even more painful the way events were forcing her to go.

Outside, they all blinked in the light, and shivered, Narinder more than the rest. It wasn't that warm a day, the sun was only a promise behind low and threatening clouds, and the familiar line of Barrier piers were more like grey thumbs sticking up than shining silver sails. In the wide, warm cabin of the launch, though, going through the gates, the general liveliness began to return; but for Narinder it was a quiet sit on a long bench, a huge sigh, and a sudden forced conversation with Paula.

"I feel really proud of that!" Narinder started, as they glided between two Barrier piers.

Paula came back from wherever she'd been herself. "Eh? Proud of what?"

"Of that." Narinder pointed at the visible parts of the huge circular gates, already covered in green to the high water mark. "This Barrier." She shifted on the bench to look at Paula. "Think of all them coaches parked next to ours. People come from all over the world to look at this – an' we can see it any old time from the top of our school, you know that?"

Paula nodded. "Yeah, I s'pose it is something."

"You *s'pose* it is?" Narinder was too loud, had to drop her oice. "Listen, girl, sometimes coming back from the cash 'n arry over Hounslow I go past the Houses of Parliament in my lad's van, past Downing Street, round Nelson – and I look at ll the people who've saved up *years* to see all that – things I can ee any old day of the week..."

"Yeah?" Paula looked surprised.

Not for the first time, Narinder felt like taking hold of her riend's shoulders and shaking the daylight out of her. "See! Even you!" she explained. "You still don't think of me as belonging here, do you? Not really. When's your birthday – August i'n it?"

Paula was listening now: definitely surprised by Narinder uddenly going off like this. "August the second," she said.

"Right! Well, mine's the first of June." Narinder let it sink in or a few seconds, stared into Paula's bewildered eyes. "Which neans I've been a Londoner two months longer than you! Never thought of that, have you?" It was one of those rare noments, with Paula staring, and slightly shaking her head. "It's still bloody hard for you to get hold of, isn't it? Same as nost of these..." Narinder waved her arm around the cabin. "What is it? This?" She jabbed a finger into the skin of her cheek. "Or this?" – waving a flat, wrapped chapati from her packed lunch.

Still Paula was staring, thinking. "I dunno," she said at last. "Both, I s'pose, bein' honest. But you're my mate!" she uddenly threw in, as if that made it all right.

Narinder felt her eyes blaze, she stabbed her fingers as she nade her painful points. "Paula, there's people that side of the river won't have nothing to do with people this side, there's the East End and South London always at one another's throats –" she dropped her voice to little more than thinking aloud – "but wouldn't they join hands quick, some of 'em, to see me shut up in that plane to Jullunder? Eh?"

Paula shrugged, tried to excuse herself from the implications of what Narinder was saying.

161

"Can't you see, Paula, I'm not here courtesy of them – or because I'm your mate. I'm here because I *belong*!"

"All right!" Paula shouted back.

"It's not courtesy of no-one! This is my Thames Barrier an' all!"

Paula laughed, the old laugh. "Oh, do leave off! You just heard how much it cost?" A try at a laugh, part of what the long friendship had always been about.

But Narinder gave it no more than a wiped smile: because somehow they were past all that, they weren't in the business of covering cracks any more. "This might be the last time I ever see it," she said, "or this dirty river, or you..." She stared as Paula closed her eyes, probably did the same with her ears as well. "'Less we crack it, Paula. 'Less you come up with the goods." For a split second, Paula was focused again, then she diverted her eyes to an apple from her bag. Narinder slid closer, made sure she made contact. "I talked to my dad last night," she told her. "I came out with it straight, I asked him what would happen if your cousin and Elkin got put into prison ..."

Paula bit into the apple. "Yeah? What he say?" she asked.

There was a silence: the chew of an apple, the sound of the tourist commentary, the showing-off of Tommy Parsons: but between the girls this huge silence. Narinder looked away and stared at the receding curves of the Thames Barrier. And when she spoke it was slowly and very quietly. "He said if they was out the way ... I wouldn't have to go." It was as if she were handling a sheet of glass so thin that it couldn't be expected to do anything but crack.

"Oh." The breath of Paula's word wouldn't have cracked a pigeon shell, though.

"But then Brian's your cousin, isn't he? He's family. My mum always says family's over on your own side – but even your best friend's a river away..."

Paula stared out of the window, down-river at the yellow

outline of a Woolwich ferry-boat. "People do get over the other side..." she said.

Narinder got up, leaned on the rail, looked down at her friend. Suddenly it seemed to her that the time for messing about with words was over. "So – you on for Saturday?" she asked. "Down the temple? Baisakhi – our big festival? *Our* chance? You can come, I've asked. Always assuming you want to..."

Again, the silence between them, then the enormous sound of Paula breathing in. "Yeah," she said, "if you like. Why not?" But her solemn face, as she looked out at the grey scene, a sugar ship still unloading, a string of barges threading down-river, hinted somehow that hopes might be quite easy to raise, like the Barrier, but it didn't happen very often for real.

Detective Inspector McNeill's office was always a place of action on a Friday evening. Everyone's diary was checked in detail, expenses were questioned as if the Inspector paid them out of his own salary, and a lot of explaining was done: but at the same time the sound of a metallic screw-top twisting off a bottle of Scotch could often be heard. This Friday, though, the air was sober and tense. A briefing had been called, and the whole of McNeill's team – his regulars and those drafted in – was gathered in the small office, frowning, smiling, dead-pan, each to his character: but waiting. If a pin were to have been heard dropping, it would have been the swish it made through the air that alerted the room, not its noisy landing.

"It's verra close, I c'n feel it," McNeill said suddenly. "Elkin's mob are watching the family, an' the family's doin' some mighty peculiar things – especially that wee lassie." They listened without moving a muscle to this man who had been chasing for so long. "So it's keep ourselves low, an' sit tight out o' sight – 'cos it's all gonna happen soon, I tell yae. It may no' be tonight, or tomorrer, but we're going' to see some converging – everything comin' together – an' when we do, we'll be converging wi' em." There were nods around the room from some of the regulars who'd been trying to nail Elkin for even longer than McNeill. "You help me get that fancy lens, an' I'll gi' ye something guid to look at. . . ." The most recent men called in, the crack drivers, looked up from the floor. "I'll gi' you the sight o' London wi'out our friend Elkin, an' that's a promise." He fixed them all, one by one, with his hard, grey stare. "But fust –" he slapped both his knees with his hands – "we watch an' we wait."

We watch an' we wait, they almost repeated, like a loyal toast. But they didn't need any of that. They had a dedication to ridding London of Elkin that had no need for words.

It was like the time she'd been in hospital, Paula thought, when she'd had her tonsils out. All the *little* things about home she'd suddenly appreciated then: like walking in and out of a room when she wanted, and eating an apple without getting someone's permission first. Now, this Friday evening, what ached her was the sight of her mother flopped in an armchair, laughing at some rubbish on the box, her dad asleep with a peaceful look on his face, and Dean sprawling all over the floor like a free-fall parachutist coming down: all these ordinary things which would change if Brian went to prison and Uncle Frank's business folded up. She closed her eyes and thought about it. For a start, her mum could never relax like this again, not with the bad name her brother would have, not with fingers pointing and all those tons of sympathetic smiles from people who were loving it. How many years would it be before Dolly Daydream could just throw her head back and laugh again? And then there was a little thing like the money she got from her job with Uncle Frank. She wouldn't find a secretary's job as well paid as that in a hurry – even supposing anyone would take her on. And where would that leave them for all their little extras now they hadn't got Grandad's money coming in? Her dad putting himself about nights as well as his long days? She opened her eyes and looked at him, snoring peacefully there: and, no, she thought, it was a hell of a lot to ask anyone, giving up all this. But wasn't that what Nindy had been asking, phoning her just now, pushing her to get the broken glasses from the temple while the festival was on tomorrow?

"Go on, you silly devil, you just said it!" Dolly was talking to a stupid contestant on the game show. "What a wallie!" She twisted round to Paula, laughing. "How do they pick 'em?"

Suddenly Paula had an overwhelming urge to go over and hug her mother. "All right, Mum?" she asked her, trying to keep the choke from her voice.

Dolly squeezed her daughter's arm. "Mustn't grumble, love," she murmured. "I miss my dad, but then – I've got everything else, haven't I? There's tons less well off than me ..." And with a little twist she hid the blink in her eye and went back to watching the television.

thirteen

That Saturday started early for Narinder. Even without her's and Paula's secret plan, when one of the days of Baisakhi fell on a Saturday she'd be expected to go – she'd *want* to go – and she'd want to look her best. It was one of those special days when the older Sikh girls wanted to dress as women, as all the Sikh boys who would sit on their fathers' side of the gurdwara wanted to look like men. This year she'd have hoped her most beautiful salvar kameez might come out, held up against the light with a hope for a warm April day, but as it was, with her best clothes packed in that suitcase on the landing, she had to settle for an old one cheered up by a filmy dupatta for her head. And a dupatta for Paula, of course – if the girl had really got the guts to turn up. She showered with some oil for her skin, put on a bit of make-up which wouldn't draw comment from her father, and gave a shine to her hair. And in the mirror, at the end of it, she was pleased and she was proud. She should definitely wear this more often, she decided: but not in India: she didn't have to go there to do that.

Her father, in another room, was damping and winding his best patka around his head, his deft fingers pulling and tucking to make the turban; while her mother, ready before either of them, was putting crisps and strong orange into a plastic bag. They were nearly ready – but there was still no sign of Paula.

Narinder went over again to the window, didn't know what to think. Had she chickened out? Had the family got to her after all? Worried now, she looked up and down the road. Just the usual parked cars and a Gas Board van, a few early shoppers hurrying to Green Street market.

"Is she coming, then? Have you called her on the telephone?" Pratap was standing smart in his best Burton suit and cracked, shiny shoes. "It's time to go or we'll miss *Akhand Path.*"

"One more minute." Narinder sighed, a deep heave which was a lot more than disappointment. It wasn't any use phoning, Paula knew all about the time. Either she was coming or she wasn't. But if she was she hadn't got long. The last thing her parents wanted to do was miss the start of Baisakhi, the ritual uncovering of the granth.

"Come on, then, please." Her father was tapping the face of his watch, another of those nervous, annoying habits he'd started doing.

"Just a minute..." But knowing in her heart now that Paula wasn't coming, had blown her out, Narinder took one last look out of the window and tidied up the net.

Hang on! Who was that? Running down the opposite pavement like a good 'un, her head twisting to the left and right before she ran out into the road? It was! It was Paula – suddenly turned up, like a bus you think you've missed! "Here she is! O.K., we can go now." Narinder picked up the spare dupatta and ran for the stairs to the shop. She'd come! So there was a chance! All right, maybe not a good one, but definitely the only one she'd got. And her heart lifted as she swirled her silk down the steep stairs.

Narinder might have felt less cheerful, though, if she'd seen the movement in the street as Paula ran along it. A burly body twisting in one car, a slight sway of the Gas Board van, and the shadow of a Kawasaki coming to a halt at the last corner the girl had turned.

At the shop door there was a fierce hug – but no special words, only polite greetings as Paula thanked Pratap for letting her come to Baisakhi, helping her this way with her R.E. homework; and within the minute they were in his car with the shop burglar alarm being switched on. A look up and down the road, and Pratap was out there to join them.

"All ready?" he asked. "Now, Paula, do you know what this festival is about. . .?"

Paula looked at him, looked at Narinder. Yes, she knew what this was all about *really*: Narinder could tell from the look on her face. The only thing no-one could be sure about was what the girl would finally make up her mind to do.

As Pratap's car pulled away the Kawasaki cruised alongside the parked Datsun Bluebird.

"It's on," Leila said. "Got to be. They're up to something, sure as eggs. An' no guesses where they're off to. So you ring Charlie and tell him to meet us at the temple in Elliott Street."

Barrett reached for his cellular car-phone. "I'll *ask* him," he corrected as he squinted at a number under the sun visor.

Leila laughed. "No, you *tell* him, she said. "Tell him from me he'll be drinking champagne with his dinner tonight! Or my name's not Leila Duke!"

It wasn't often that Mick turfed passengers out: only when they were sick-drunk sometimes. But this Saturday morning he had to do it; very politely, and after calling up a mate to pick up the fare. Then he drove fast to a phone and made the urgent call home Dolly had had him radioed to make. "What's up, Doll? What the 'ell's goin' on?"

She hadn't even got the number out. "Mick, it's Paula. She's gone!"

"Gone – gone where?" Mick let the kiosk door close, stared down the phone.

"Round Narinder's she said. But it doesn't smell right, Mick. She's left a note. . ."

"What's it say?"

"Listen. 'Whatever I make my mind up to do, I want you to know it's for the best.' Mick, I don't like the sound of that. She was definitely 'off' last night, very funny. It's like she's. . ." Dolly's voice broke up; there were seconds while she got herself

ound to bringing it out. "It's like she's ... running away, or
something. You read about these teenagers, turns out you
don't know 'em. Mick..."

Mick swore, swung round in the kiosk as if he suddenly
thought he might be being watched, lowered his voice as if that
would keep things tighter. "Doll, love, I *know* what this is all
about. An' she ain't running off, honest to God. Now just do
what I say. Get Frank, quick, he'll only be up the showroom,
tell him to call for you, straightaway, an' meet me round the
printer's, the girl's place. We'll see if we can't pick up their
tracks ..."

"All right, Mick." She opened her mouth to say something
else, but he'd already put the phone down; and almost before
the kiosk door had closed the cab was halfway through a
U-turn back to Pratap's printing shop.

With the sun on the kameez, the saris and the dupattas,
picking out their gold and silver threads, the light Punjabi
clothing seemed to come into its own. The cautious still wore
coats and cardigans, and very few of the men were in white,
preferring the warmth of western dress, but the turbans also
shone and steel karas glittered on wrists as the two-handed
greetings were given. The girls got out of Pratap's car. It all
seemed so natural and right, Narinder thought, even in Elliott
Street: even in a gurdwara which had once been a working
men's club. More, it was what she knew, and what they were
here about, what they were here to try to stop her losing. She
glanced at Paula. There was no knowing what was going on
behind her tense, tight face, staring up, too, at the big building.
But it was all very choking, and one way and another Narinder
had no eyes for anything else.

She certainly didn't notice anyone in the cars parked along
the street, nor the coincidence of another Gas Board van at the
kerb; and she had no ears for the faint sound of a large
motor-bike coming.

Pratap led his party inside: turned right to the langar where Kamal needed to leave the food she'd brought. Narinder watched Paula taking everything in: saw her back go rigid as they went into the kitchen.

"This it?" she whispered. "This what used to be the committee room?" But her doubts were obvious as she frowned at the women standing round the hot-plate cooking chapatis, at the long work-top where sandwiches were being cut, at the sink where the washing up was being done.

"No, 'course not. This is where we eat. Anyone coming in gets given food: an' today there's everyone, all the kids ..." She looked at Paula in her *Lacoste* track-suit with the dupatta over her head. East and West. And it suited her; somehow they went well together. And catching Paula's eye she held it, there in the middle of the busy room: because there was one thing now over which there couldn't be any compromise, no dodging the issue.

It was either, or ... A straight choice.

"You made up your mind yet, Paula?" she asked her quietly. "What *are* you gonna do if we get that thing? Give it in – or give it back?"

"Eh?" Not for the first time Paula sounded as if she were deliberately acting dumb. But without knowing, Kamal chose that moment to ask her almost the same question.

"Chapatis, Paula?" she asked her. "Or would you rather be eating sandwiches?"

There was a moment of silence between the three in the middle of the noisy langar. Paula looked at Narinder and her mother, at the chapatis and the cut loaves. "I dunno, Mrs Sidhu," she said at last. "That's my trouble, I reckon. I can't make up my mind about anything."

Outside, Charlie Elkin, still in his Saturday morning track-suit and trainers, was driving along Elliott Street and parking his Mercedes; while back outside Pratap's printing shop Mick had

170

ıst finished talking to the woman next door and was running
ack across the pavement to Dolly and Frank.

"Something's blowin' all right! Old girl reckons they've
one up their church, our Paula an' all. What'd that be?" he
sked his brother-in-law, "the mosque up Elliott Street?"

"Yeah, would be, Micky. I don't know any others..."

"Come on then, no time to hang about."

It was a matter of minutes to the gurdwara, the speed they
oth went, then pulling up and parking a street apart. But it
as Mick who got his cab into the prime spot just outside the
ain doors, the way cabbies do, and who had to wait
npatiently for the others to run along to him.

"What you reckon, then?" he asked.

But Frank hadn't heard him. He was standing back by the
erb and just staring up at the big, yellow-brick building.
Here, Micky," he said slowly, light dawning, "I've tumbled
ow, son – you know what this place is, don't you? You do,
oll!"

And Dolly was nodding vigorously, a strong movement
hich just about held back the tears. "It's the old Working
Ien's Club. Our dad's old club. Used to bring us here as kids
..."

"Knew it like the back of his hand," Frank murmured. "All
e little nooks and crannies ... Christ!" He suddenly slapped
is leg. "He played it bloomin' clever, old Dad – he knew Elkin
ouldn't dream of looking in a Sikh temple, not in a million
ears!"

And now Mick's eyes had lit up, too. "I get you. He came
d hid it in here. *And Paula knows.*" He stared at Dolly, all
ide eyes. "And now she's come to find it. That's what her
ote was goin' on about. What she's gonna do with it!"

Frank moved himself. "Right!" he said. "Micky, you keep
 eye on the front. Dolly, wait down by my car, keep the
gine going." He threw her the keys. "I'll check the back –
d keep your heads down, both of you. 'Cos you can bet

McNeill's not week-ending in Scotland: not if he's the bloke
reckon he is. . . " And looking for all the world like someone u
to no good, he hurried round the narrow path to the back of th
building.

In the corridor outside the main hall of the gurdwara a
Narinder could see were bent backs: men, women and childre
taking off their shoes and putting them in places where the
knew they'd find them, counting along, 'three up from th
sandals' sort of thing. She did the same, and nudged Paula t
take off hers, too. "Hope you washed your feet!" But Prata
shushed her. This festival started the Sikh year, and had to b
taken very seriously. His own socks were smart and withou
pattern, new for the occasion. She looked round at all the othe
socks and the tights. Would be bare feet in India, she though
Dusty, bare feet. And again she tried to read something o
Paula's face. Would she or wouldn't she help to get that ler
when the moment came? And would she or wouldn't she war
it handed over to the police? But from her expression, from he
sad eyes and her set mouth it was impossible to tell: Narinde
had never seen a face so closed, so tight.

At least Paula had *come* to the temple, though; she coul
easily have stayed at home and left it all down to her. And, "I
this it?" she was suddenly asking. Narinder looked to wher
she was pointing, to a door at the top of the narrow flight c
stairs just outside the main hall.

"Yeah. I reckon. 'Bout the only place it can be. It's where w
keep the holy book. Would've been the committee room
must've been." Narinder felt relieved. At least the girl was sti
thinking about it.

But Pratap was steering them through the double doors, an
with backward glances and a stolen stare at each other, the
had to go with him.

Now that she knew what it had been before, Narinder sav
the main room of the gurdwara through slightly different eyes

she saw how it would once have been a big concert hall, probably filled with rows and rows of those metal and canvas chairs, all facing the stage: because you could see where the curtains would have run, and the steps down off the platform on either side. It was a long way from being an old-fashioned music hall now, though: there was a world of difference in the way the place was used. The stage was still there, but it was just a raised area these days where the bright canopy was set for the granthi to sit under and chant from the book on its big cushion. And in front of it, where the seats would have been, everyone sat on the bare floor which was all covered in white sheeting.

Without a word, her father led them to put coins in the collecting box and kiss the floor, then he went to sit on the right of the temple with the men; while her mother made to lead them near the front on their left.

"We'll keep out the way," Narinder whispered. "We'll stay up the back." It wasn't the place for a row or even a noisy discussion. Kamal shrugged and went forward; while Narinder found a space for the two of them as far back as she could, in easy reach of the door.

They were only just in time. The hall was filling up, but before any more could come in from the corridor, the granth on its cushion was carried head-high from the granth-room up those stairs, and within minutes *Akhand Path* had begun – the granth uncovered from its ornate cloth and the people, the whole Khalsa, singing to the accompaniment of tabla and harmoniums.

Narinder looked across at her father; he was totally engrossed in this special kirtan, one hundred per cent of him. And she couldn't see her mother for the people in between. Everyone was concentrating to the front. So! This was the moment, then: what they'd been waiting for. It wouldn't be better. This was when they found out if all the braille business had been right, if Paula's grandad had hidden the evidence

173

well enough not to have been found by someone – and yet easy enough for her and Paula to put their hands on it. Not all that hopeful, when you suddenly thought about things like that.

The tabla were sending out their rhythms, the harmoniums their tune, and the people were singing: "*There exists but one God who is called the True, the Creator, free from fear and hate, immortal, not begotten, self-existent, great and compassionate.*"

"Come on!" Narinder hissed at Paula. "Now's best. . ." And crouching low, winking for their silence at a couple of girls she knew, she slid herself and Paula out through the big double doors into the corridor among the rows and rows of waiting shoes; didn't see two elders watching them go. Now the girls' eyes were on one place only: on the narrow flight of stairs that led up to the room where the granth was kept: the holy of holies: the old committee room. They looked up the stairs, and they looked at one another, Narinder heard Paula swallow. And she did the same. With the chanting coming from the gurdwara and the rows of obedient shoes watching out here, it did seem like some huge sort of abuse to be going up into the room where the granth was kept.

"Can't just go in there, can we?" All at once Paula seemed to be looking for an out.

"Not s'posed to." But Narinder wasn't going to give in: no, this close to finding out whether they'd got the braille message right and whether that lens was still there. On silent socks she moved up the stairs, turned to make sure Paula was following. But the girl hadn't moved, was still a way back from the foot. "You on, are you?" she asked her. "You're not. . . ?"

And that seemed to do it. Being flapped at like a write-off suddenly pulled Paula up. "No, 'course not – " she said. "Go on, then!"

Narinder led the way to the top of the stairs, her dupatta hitched back from her ears so that she could listen for the sounds of someone coming. But apart from the chanting there was just the swish of her own clothes and the breathing of the girl behind her. Nervously, she laid a hand on the brass door-knob at the top: she gripped it, twisted it – and pushed.

The door opened easily. It didn't grate, didn't squeak, and no alarm sounded; it opened up obligingly for her and allowed her a squint inside. The room was empty. Swiftly, Narinder pulled Paula in and closed the door.

"Whooo!"

It was quite a room, small with the end walls lined in pine and the others plastered. Glittering decorations like those downstairs hung from the ceiling, and up on a table sat a smaller version of the other granth canopy, all beautifully decorated in bright colours – but empty now, like an ornate bed from which a guru has risen. The girls took it all in quickly, their necks twisting about as they searched for something which had been there much longer than all this.

"Look, over there!" Narinder pointed to the long wall on the return where the door had opened. It was there, the fire, a *New World* gas appliance, its stainless steel all speckled where the years had got at it. But had anything else got at it as well – a hand or a duster or a broom? Narinder dived for the fire and started groping under it in the space left for the draught. Pushing from her mind any nasty thoughts of spiders and mice she blindly felt for what else might be under there. And Paula was there, too, poking in where the control was, running a finger along the burners. A single lens could be anywhere, they knew.

"Oh!" Narinder stifled a small scream. What was that? Her fingers had found something cold and soft and curled. They shot back off it. A *dead* something, it had to be!

"What is it?"

"Dunno. Hold on." Bravely, Narinder forced her fingers back to it, she pulled a face and arched away as she made herself probe the something out. With a flick she sent it skidding onto the lino floor. "Uuggh!" It *was* something dead, wasn't it? Black, wrinkled, covered with dust. And she'd touched it . . . !

Paula was on her knees looking very closely at it, hands well away. But, "Yeah!" she suddenly said. "Nindy! Gloves!"

"Gloves? That all?" Narinder was under the fire again, feeling desperately now for anything else. FIRE, COMMITTEE ROOM, ELLIOTT STREET. If the lens really wasn't here then the thing had been found by somebody. And if it had been found she was finished. Without the evidence to put Elkin and Brian away it was goodbye to London and definitely the end of the life she'd known. Without the lens, Paula didn't even have anything to make up her mind about. "Leave them old gloves, come on and help!" She was desperate. This was the end of the line.

But Paula was blowing dust off the gloves, picking up the rolled leather. "I knew! They're Grandad's!" she said in triumph. "I knew it!"

"Honest?!" So what was in them? Narinder came away from the fire and tried to help Paula unroll the old leather. But before either of them could get a finger into the lining, could feel whether the gloves were empty or not, the sounds of deep Punjabi could be heard, men's voices – and they were coming up the granth room stairs...

"Quick!" Narinder pushed the gloves into Paula's palm and almost threw her across the room, behind where the door would open. Herself, she stood well back but in full view, took up a position where it looked as if she were simply admiring the silks of canopy. Like that, they froze. And two men came in, elderly Sikhs in full white suits and with the bare feet of India.

"A girl?" one of them said in Punjabi. "What are you doing here?" And as Narinder delayed answering, made the men advance towards her to see if her hands had done some damage to the silks, Paula slid round the door and flew in a sudden billow of dupatta down the steep stairs.

From the gurdwara the voices, the tabla, the harmoniums went on celebrating Baisakhi; from the granth room the angry voices upbraided Narinder; but there in the passage were only the silent shoes and no-one taking any notice whatever of the scared white girl. Breathing heavily with the fright, Paula looked round. She saw her own shoes, as familiar to her feet as those gloves she was holding had been to her grandad's hands. And without a backward glance she quickly slipped her shoes on and walked out into the sunshine of Elliott Street.

fourteen

Paula didn't know what her next move was going to be. But
finding somewhere quiet to see what was in the gloves had got
to be high on the list. So what about shooting round the
cemetery, she thought, before someone came after her? Or
should she hang about down the road in case Nindy came
running out in a minute? Afterwards, that was five seconds'
wondering she forgot she'd ever done because things happened
so quickly, so frighteningly – starting with the sudden rev of a
Kawasaki vibrating the air, and her head whipping round to
see these black leathers coming straight at her along the
pavement, someone crazy racing the machine tight to the wall
to cut her off from diving back into the gurdwara. In a panic
she swung round the other way to see this big man sprinting at
her from the opposite direction. Three sides cut off – and there
was no doubt who they were coming for! In terror she stared
out into the street, went to run for the houses on the other side.
She could scream! She could knock a door down! Except there
was a stupid cab in her way, and it was moving, closing down
the gap. . .

"Paula!"

No! It was her dad's voice, her dad's cab. With a leap she
threw herself desperately at the rear door, just as the motor-
bike screeched to a swerving stop at her heels and as the big
man grabbed at what she'd got in her hand.

Paula screamed "Quick!" The big grab missed and she
threw herself onto the rubber floor of the cab. And Mick's foot
was already down as she reached out for the swinging door to
slam it shut. He pulled out into the traffic lane and clattered
the cab away down the street. Paula pressed her face at the

rear-view window: saw the rider in leathers trying to kick-start the motor-bike, saw her Uncle Frank come charging round from the back of the gurdwara, saw Elkin in his Mercedes coming after the cab. "Oh God!" she shouted. Everyone was on to her now.

"You got it? Them glasses?" Mick asked, swinging the vehicle violently round a cyclist.

"Hold on ..." Fumbling, fighting to keep her balance, Paula unrolled the gloves, turned them inside out: but her fingers knew before her eyes that there was definitely something there. This wasn't just a pair of her poor old grandad's gloves. This was it. This was the evidence that everyone was after – Elkin's glasses, or half of them, a thick, bifocal lens in a stub of gold frame. "Yeah," she said, "yeah, it's it." She re-rolled the gloves, pressed herself back to the rear window. Now Elkin was right behind, staring up at her from his car, and the rider in leathers – the woman from the ferry – was up front with him and looking every bit as if she'd carry out her death threat. And they were gaining, could cut them off in seconds.

"Quick! Go on! I gotta think!"

"*Think*?" Mick went round something else, made them hit their heads on the cab roof as he bounced off a traffic island. "What's to think about? I've only got the king of the East End up my back!" But he weaved some more. And now Paula could pick out the other vehicles in the mad chase, Uncle Frank's car, someone else's behind him, and two gas vans going like the clappers along the wrong side of the road, trying to overtake everything.

"Eh? What's to think about? We can't mess about with him!"

Paula screwed round to the front. The trouble was, she *couldn't* think. Who could make their mind up what to do in the middle of a car chase when the next second you could be slung out through a window? All she could do right now was hang on.

Up front was a crossroads where Mick had right of way. Get

across here, she thought, and ... But she didn't really know what they could do: everyone was so tight to them. And suddenly, out from either side of the junction came two more gas vans, big ones, racing to make a road block. No! Paula shut her eyes, braced herself for the crash. But there was room, a gap just wide enough somehow, and Mick went shooting through it.

"They gone mad? Christ! That's the law!" Mick's face said he didn't believe this was going on. But he kept his foot down. The trouble was, the Mercedes had got through, too, had somehow squeezed through the same gap when the vans were forced to stop: and now it was up alongside, Elkin bumping the cab, forcing it over with loud blasts on its horns and the woman's face twisted in angry shouts.

"I've had this!" Mick shouted. "I'm stopping 'fore someone gets killed." And with a sudden and loud squeal of rubber on kerb he jerked the cab to a stop.

"No!" But Paula was out before the cab had stopped. There were streets, gardens, places she could go. Just somewhere to go to think – think with the lens in her hand. She definitely had to have more time. With her head down, she shot across the road, while car doors slammed, people shouted. "*Come here! Come here with that!*" But she took no notice, went on running, scared, blindly, because she knew she wasn't ready to put that lens in anyone's hand yet: no-one's, not Elkin's and not McNeill's. Too much hung on it to do it in a rush. Before, it had all been *just suppose*: now she'd got the thing in her hand it was for real, and she had to be *sure*.

She ran at a kerb, swung round a road-sign, and suddenly she realised where she was. The ferry. Without knowing it the chase had taken her to the river – and all at once here she was running round by the wall which led to the boat. Oh God, no! Cut off! Because there was no turning back, not from here. Elkin was behind her, she knew he was, she could hear the squeal of his trainers, and he'd have her if she tried to double back, make a dash for the foot tunnel which ran under the water.

But wouldn't he have her anyway? Wasn't that the ferry pulling out, and the vehicle road lifting away from the deck? So what to do? Stop? Or was there a wild half chance? Paula didn't break step to think. Head down, on she ran, ducking under the barrier-pole, her feet drumming on the wooden planks as she hit the ramp and made a crazy charge for the departing ferry-boat. People were yelling but she couldn't hear them now. Elkin was shouting something, and her dad; but she ran on towards the thin air, and as the gap between the boat-deck and the ramp got wider by the second, still tightly clutching the gloves, she went for the ferry in a desperate one-footed leap.

The gap was wide, and the drop was, too: ten metres down and two out: but she made it, hurt the balls of her feet, jolted her back, but she hardly even stumbled. A deck-hand swore at her; she took no notice, was too busy running to the far end of the car deck in case Elkin was jumping, too. But as she gulped in lungs-full of the cold, salty air, a quick look round told her that he hadn't tried it. He was running in the other direction, heading for the foot tunnel instead. Oh, God, no! Her heaving shoulders drooped. So she hadn't got away, then; because running under the tunnel was a lot quicker than the boat. People on foot never bothered waiting for a ferry when they were in a rush. And with Elkin's speed he'd beat this boat across and have tons of time to get his breath back by the time she got there.

So that was it! Heart pumping Paula looked out over the rail and sighed. She just wasn't going to have the time she wanted for thinking. Five minutes, that'd be about it: five minutes at the most to make her mind up on one of the most difficult decisions she'd ever have to make in her life. Her friend, or her family: that was what it came down to: and without any easy, middle road answer to make it a bit fair on both, either.

But at least she did still *have* a choice, she thought. All right,

Elkin might be waiting on the other side of the water, but h could never search the whole of this ferry-boat for something a small as a lens, especially with the law so close behind him. S she only had to hide it, and then tell McNeill where it was: o give it to one of these drivers with a message, because Elki wouldn't actually kill her with so many people about, woul he?

And he definitely wouldn't if she just made him happy b handing it over to him, she told herself.

There in the sun on the car deck, plunged into the gloom o this awful decision, she walked about blind, saw everything bu saw nothing, nervously fingered her grandad's proudly-mad necklace almost as if she needed it to remind her who she was her mum's daughter, her uncle's niece . . . and Narinder Kau Sidhu's best friend.

The ferry-boat, *The Ernest Bevin*, was almost in mid-stream pausing to let a string of empty barges track up river. Paul came back to the rail again, looked back at the north ban where her father was, and Uncle Frank, and where a flashin light and the arrival of people in blue suddenly said tha everything was happening. Which meant the crooks woul stay clear, if they'd got any sense, and she'd have a receptio committee when she got back from Elkin. She looked this wa and that, tried to make the swing of her head help her to forc an answer out. Did she still have any choice, then – supposin she could ever make one? She kicked the layered paint of th bulkhead. There was nothing to force her hand, to make her d anything. Entirely down to her, it was – all in her lap.

Squeezing and unsqueezing the balled glove, Paula looke at her reflection in the car beside her. The river wind wa blowing her hair all ways, was keeping the red-running roug on her face – while the fright in her own eyes definitely scare her stiff. She breathed in and out deeply till the cold air hur her windpipe. And softly, she swore – as her eyes changed thei focus at something on the car almost as familiar as her ow ace: the sticker on the window she'd been staring at; the ticker no-one ever seemed to want to scrape off. *Frank Butler Motors*: the sign with the address and the phone number where her mother worked, the contacts for times of trouble which Paula knew by heart. Dolly Prescott! Her mum! And there in he wind Paula could almost hear her answering the phone in her posh business voice; till her throat suddenly lumped up at he picture of her mum sitting in her armchair the night before, her home voice talking back at the telly while she squeezed her arm and told her she was all right. *Mustn't grumble, love. I miss my dad, but then – I've got everything else, haven't I? There's tons less well off than me . . .* Oh, sugar! They were right. It would hit her so bad if the lens got turned in. Uncle Frank would lose out on everything, sister Dolly's good job would go with it, and everyone in Shepherd's Gate would point their fingers at the lodgy family where the daughter turned them in. It was true, Paula thought miserably. Like her dad had said: *This is our family hanging in the balance. Doesn't that come first?* They were words she'd never forget.

There was a ringing of bells and Paula felt a sudden judder, a change in the engines; the forward motion of the ferry-boat seemed to have halted as the screws began to back-wash and all at once the vessel was changing direction, was going back to the northern shore! The sun and the wind were coming at Paula's face from the other side. They were going back, she thought, going back to save her from Elkin. They'd radioed the captain and given him police orders: it was all being taken out of her hands.

She started to panic. So how did that change things? Did that mean she couldn't still help her family? Did it mean she couldn't get the lens to one of the gang?

Passengers were staring up out of their cars; a deck-hand was going round telling them there was a bit of a panic going on, and she heard someone say, "Bomb-scare." In the end, just to look away from all the scared idiots who had nothing in the world to be afraid of, Paula stared over the side at the churning wake. And suddenly it struck her. There *was* something else she could do. She could chuck the lens in the river where no-one could ever get it. And if no-one could ever get it, no-one could ever use it as evidence against Elkin.

Paula looked up, looked out, relieved to have an answer at last. But even as she did so, as she stared up-river, she saw the piers of the Thames Barrier glinting in the sun. And having thought she'd made up her mind Paula's heart sank. *This is my Thames Barrier an' all! I've been a Londoner two months longer than you, Paula. Ever thought of that?* They were words she'd never forget, too. And it was true. Nindy had been. She'd got just as much right to be here as anyone. Which meant that Elkin and his lot forcing her to go away was like forcing the Prescotts to move to Australia – just to get away.

Miserably, Paula leaned on the rail. They were getting closer to the north bank. She could see their faces, everyone waiting for her: her dad, her mum, her Uncle Frank; the police and, right at the far end of the ramp three people who looked a lot like Nindy and her family.

Oh, God! So what did she do, apart from jumping in the river herself – which that minute didn't seem such a crazy idea. There was no-one she could ask, was there? No-one here, no-one alive. She looked up at the sky, the scudding clouds, the patches of blue. So what would Grandad have done? she suddenly started saying to herself as the tears came.

It *was* Narinder standing at the ferry approach. After the upset in the gurdwara her father had had to come out of the service for her to be handed over to him by the Sikh elders. And it had just been the way it happened that, as he'd taken her to the street for a strong word, they'd seen the tail-end of the chase and gone after it. And now, seeing the girl on the boat Narinder knew what was still in Paula's hand; standing there at the ferry she would have known what it was even if all the

184

alk hadn't been about it, all the stuff with the squad car radios and Paula's people muttering, all about those gloves.

She shivered as she looked across at the little crowd of people the police had brought up from the tunnel, lounging and smoking as if no-one could really touch them. But as the ferry-boat swung round and came towards them, all Narinder had eyes for was Paula. All she had to do was just bring these gloves ashore, because Elkin's people couldn't touch her with all these police around. All Paula had to do now was walk off and give them in, and then she would know that she was safe to stay. Elkin would go to prison and so would a lot of the others, and all his rotten rackets would go with him. And then her dad would be free to go on running his business, and she could go on living her own life.

Everybody there was watching, not just Narinder. No-one was talking any more. Even the gang had stopped looking everywhere else. Silently, with just the sound of the river, they all watched Paula being brought into the shore. But as they all watched, even as Narinder thought she knew what Paula was going to do, as her heart rose at the prospect of the lens being given to that policeman in charge, her disbelieving eyes saw Paula slowly raise her right arm over the rail, unroll what was in her hand and, with a flick, skate her wrist out over the water, casting what she'd been holding into the wake of the ferry-boat. For a second the leather danced, and then disappeared forever.

"She's thrown it. Good girl, she's got rid of it!" Paula's dad didn't seem to care who heard, not now that the evidence had gone. He danced, hugged her mother, kissed her, shook the other man's hand and gave one of those long nodding looks over at the people being watched, who were suddenly not lounging but standing up straight, and all smiles. Narinder saw the policeman kick a car tyre and walk to a radio in one of the vans. And finally she saw Paula, her head in her hands on the rail, crying out her heart.

Narinder was numb. One of those stomach-churning feel ings surged through her, and then she felt nothing: didn't nod nor shake her head when her father asked her in Punjabi if that wasn't what she'd expected. "Innocent, guilty, right or wrong, Narinder: they're white, aren't they? They're all the same colour . . ."

Her face set like a hardened mask, suddenly feeling closer to that suitcase in her hall and so much further away from the girl coming in on the ferry, Narinder watched the vessel dock. She saw the slow lowering of the ramp, the cars staying still on the vehicle deck, and just the one passenger raising herself up of the rail and pulling herself away to walk ashore.

No-one went to meet her, not even her mother and father, not at first, anyway. There seemed to be a sadness on Paula which Paula, on her own, had got to bring to them. Just the first few steps. And then her dad ran for her and put an arm round her shoulder. But Narinder watched her shake him off as if she definitely didn't want to be cuddled, not by him or by her mother or by her uncle. She didn't even seem to want to stop. She just kept coming on off that ferry and up the ramp with the tears pouring wet all down her face. There was no way she could manage a smile, nor even a turn of her head. And they dropped away, her family, as if they guessed what she was doing, coming to say sorry to the one she'd just let down. And they seemed to respect it, and let her come.

Narinder straightened her back. She didn't know what she'd say, what she'd do. On Paula came, up towards her, still crying, her shoulders shaking badly as her breath kept catch ing, her fist clenched tight with the tension of what she was going to say. But as she got up to her, as Narinder suddenly knew what she'd say back, the girl only hesitated, didn't even look at her, just went on past; that same, slow sad pace as if she was walking back into the East End to lose herself for ever.

Only when she got to the end, to where the ferry road met the ordinary street did Paula stop. And there with a half turn to her right she walked over to McNeill. Narinder stared, thought she'd die with her heart not beating. Because, gradually opening her clenched fist, Paula slowly revealed something transparent, and something gold in her hand. And all the East End heard what she said.

"I didn't want to ... see my grandad's gloves ... up in court," she told him. "This'll do, won't it?"

McNeill looked at what she was holding out. "Aye," he said, and very carefully he took Elkin's lens and gold arm from the wet hand which seemed itself to have been crying. "This'll do a treat, girl."

Gently the policeman led Paula back to her shattered family, to whom she knew herself she could say nothing: not a word: but to whom over the days to come she might try to explain something about her grandad's bravery in protecting them all from Elkin so that they could go on leading their own lives: and how the only answer she could find in the end was to think about the old man, and make up her mind to do the same for Narinder: praying, all the while, that they'd be brave with her – even when the money was short, and the fingers pointed, and the words of abuse were heard.

HIGH PAVEMENT BLUES
Bernard Ashley

Misery for 15-year-old Kevin means setting up his mother's market stall on a bleak Saturday morning to the taunts of Alfie Cox and his dad on the pitch next door. Kevin has to do something about it. But what?

EASY CONNECTIONS
Liz Berry

Cathy's vision of the future is shattered when she meets Paul Devlin, the lead guitarist with the rock group Easy Connection and a millionaire superstar. A powerful love story.

ARE YOU LISTENING, KAREN?
David Day

Jay Border is sixteen and shy – and hopelessly in love. Desperate for a sympathetic ear, he sets off to have a long chat with Karen, his sister, now dead. A moving account of adolescent insecurities.

CLOUDY/BRIGHT
John Rowe Townsend

A sensitive and amusing contemporary love story about two young aspiring photographers. The same events are related alternately by Sam and Jenny, often from very different angles!

JOHNNY JARVIS
Nigel Williams

On one level a tough thriller, this is also a study of our times – a hauntingly sad account of what it is like to be an out-of work, no-hope teenager today.

THE SCARECROWS
Robert Westall

A gripping novel of menace and suspense that brings a boy and his family to the brink of destruction.

THE FORTUNATE FEW
Tim Kennemore

Jodie Bell is a professional gymnast – starved to the perfect weight, worked to the point of collapse and sold to the highest bidder. A thought-provoking story set in the not-too-distant future.

NO PLACE LIKE
Gene Kemp

Peter Williams has problems – he fails exams, demolishes bathroom walls, and almost burns the house down. And just when he finally seems to be settling down at sixth form college, trouble looms once again . . .

PROVE YOURSELF A HERO
K. M. Peyton

Kidnapping is a terrifying enough experience itself, but Jonathan finds that his eventual release causes him even greater problems!